BRINLIN
FOREST

BOOKS BY ROBIN STEPHEN

Chronicles of the Tessilari
Tessili Academy
Tessili Rogue
Tessili Revenge

Annals of the Brinlocks
Brinlin Isle
Brinlin Forest
Brinlin Cove

Brinlin Forest

Annals of the Brinlocks: Book II

A Story of Bydaira

Robin Stephen

This is a work of fiction. All characters, events, and organization portrayed in this novel are either product's of the author's imagination or are used fictitiously.

BRINLIN FOREST

Copyright © 2018 by Brown Wing Press

robinstephen.com

ISBN 978-1-946238-01-6 (ebook)
ISBN 978-1-946238-04-7 (print)

Cover design by Robin Deutschendorf
Maps by Robin Deutschendorf

Brown Wing Press
Iowa City, IA
brownwingpress.com

First Brown Wing Press Edition

This little series is dedicated to the wonderful teachers I had in 3rd, 4th, 5th, and 6th grade who went out of their way to show an interest in my youthful scribblings. It's impossible to overstate the vast impact so much early support and valuable feedback had on my desire to keep writing, and get better at it.

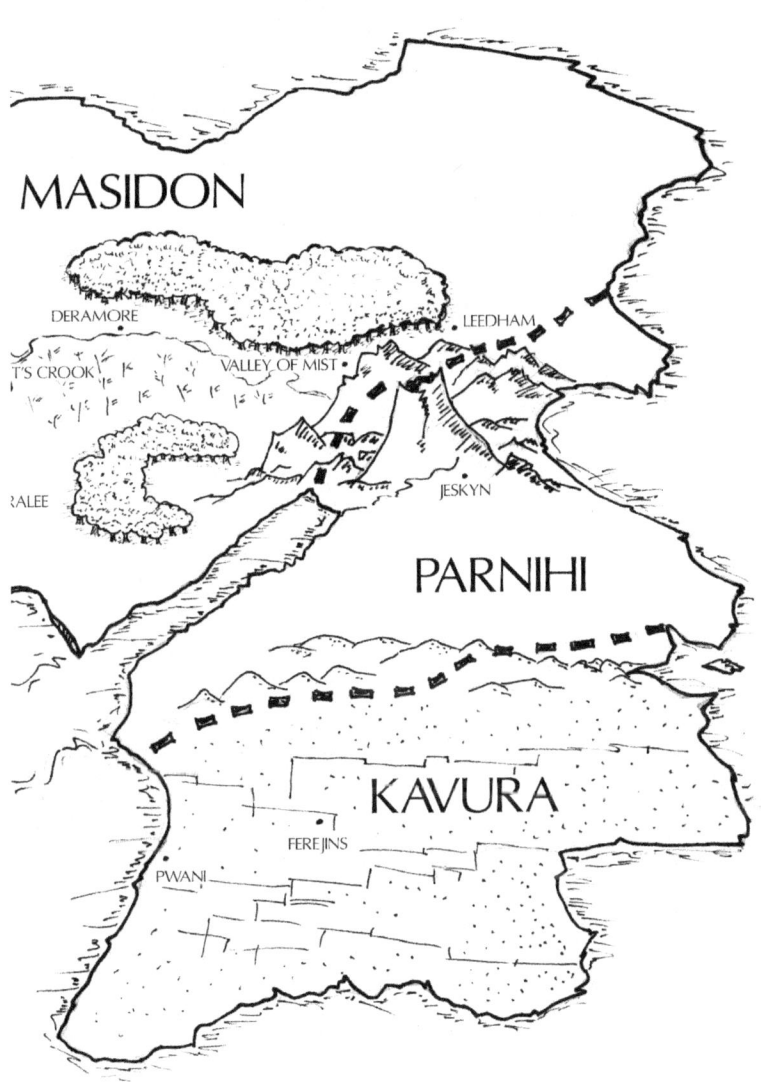

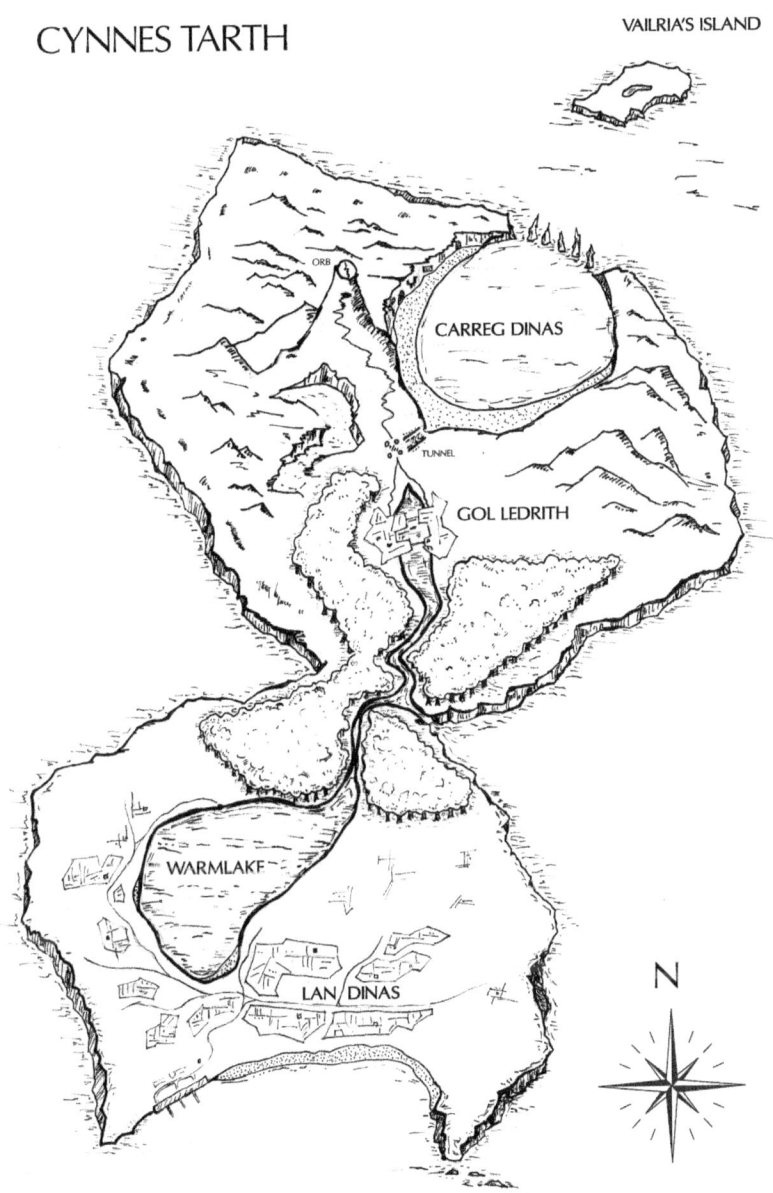

PRELUDE

Marim stumbled down the hill, her sea bag heavy on her shoulder and her thoughts a wild scramble. Kix's emotions, intense but muddled, made her own blood boil with a directionless thirst for revenge. *Why is he so angry? Revenge for what?*

She had no time to sort it out, no time to try to understand. The sight of the ship drifting slowly away from the quay seemed to replay in her mind, the captain staring down from his place at the rail. He'd seen her, and it had made no difference.

She was stranded. But worse, according to Cockram, the mob she'd seen on her way up to the harbor was hunting *her*.

The smart thing to do would be to get out of Lan Dinas. She had her bag back now, her tablets, spellbook, food, extra clothing. She could go to the forest everyone was so afraid of. Kix could learn to hunt rabbits and small game. She could carve out an isolated life beneath the trees, at least until the simmering hatred in this place came down from a boil.

But Marim had a bad habit of not doing the smart thing.

Cockram was heading for Embriem's. The woman in the shifting cloak was following him. Marim was following the woman.

In the darkness, hurrying down the narrow track, Marim tried to make a complete list of facts – things she knew about her situation without a doubt. *I am stranded among people who believe I am an abomination.*

It was not a promising start to her list. Before she could get any further, Embriem's house came into view. Marim stopped short, arrested with the force of her surprise.

The mob was there, filling the space between the road and Embriem's stately mansion. Many carried torches. Others carried primitive weapons, like pitchforks and the strange, barbed hooks used to harvest reeds. She remembered the angry muttering she'd overheard, the dark energy that seemed to writhe and coil among these people, pushing them on. *There are so many of them,* she thought. *So many people who hate me.*

If these people were here on Embriem's doorstep, angry, looking for vengeance, it was because of Marim. She stood in the shadows on the other side of the road, quivering with uncertainty. If any one of these people saw her, that dark energy would take over. Would they kill her? Did they hate her so much as that?

She remembered the spark in Cockram's eye, the way he'd tried to stop her on the road, Kix's sudden thirst for revenge. *Revenge for what?*

Marim's body seemed to remember what her mind could not. Her throat felt suddenly tight, her breathing growing shallow and laborious. She seemed to remember kneeling in the wet fog, listening to the sound of a scuffle. Kix's angry cry, a man's scream.

The thoughts faded. On the edge of the crowd, Marim saw the two figures she'd been following. The man, Cockram, had stopped to stare at the assembled group of people as well. The woman, with her carved staff and shifting cloak, stood behind him. Up on the road, she'd thought them enemies. Now, she noticed a certain similarity between them – the way they both stood with their weight on their heels, the lift of the chin, the set of the shoulders.

Even as she puzzled about this, the man suddenly surged to life. He spun on the woman, holding something small and silver in his hand. *Is that a stunrod?*

Black memories rose up from the depths of Marim's mind. She seemed to feel again the blank shock, the fuzzing pain that made her whole body seize into paralysis.

Before, Marim had been confused and scared, but also a little bit curious.

Now, she was terrified.

As she watched the man's quick, lashing blow, she saw the woman was not ready. She'd be hit, for sure, and she would fall just as Marim had fallen so often beneath the stunrod Nylan had used against her.

Who is this man? The fear had a sharp grip on her stomach now. *What have I overlooked about this place?*

CHAPTER 1

Braven lounged on a moss-covered boulder, strumming his lute and singing quietly to himself. All around, the forest was a massive, silent presence. The trunks of the great trees stood like stately pillars, their crowns lost in the dimming fog. The leaves were down this time of year, the branches bare and gray, but the ever-present ferns still brought a splash of green to the forest floor.

The moss was damp, of course. Everything in the forest was damp. This didn't matter to Braven. All of his clothing was resistant to the wet, kept fresh by a delicate drying spell woven into the fabric, and the fog was always warm. So he played in relative comfort, his fingers dancing over humming strings.

As it wouldn't do for cheerful lute music to be heard anywhere in the enchanted forest, Braven maintained a spell as he played his song. There wasn't a name for the spell. It was something he'd come up with on his own. He held it around himself so it distorted the notes of his light-hearted tune into the vague murmurings of spectral voices and the snarling growls of dires – the sorts of things the people of Lan Dinas would expect to hear if anyone gathered the courage to venture into the woods.

Keeping the forest creepy was Braven's job. He was good at it. He wasn't good at playing the lute, which was why he mostly did it out here where no one could hear.

He was nearing the end of the song when he felt the little buzz in his sternum that meant someone had crossed one of his perimeter lines. He stopped singing, cocking his head to listen while maintaining a quiet strum with his fingers. But he couldn't hear a thing.

Rising, Braven tucked his lute with his pack into the hollow at the base of the ancient tree behind him. Then he adjusted his cloak and strode off to see who'd tripped his alarm.

He didn't move with any particular urgency. In all his years working the woods, Braven could count on one hand the number of times he'd come across anyone other than a wary woodsman. He wasn't expecting anything untoward, so when the voices drifted back to him on the dim air, he froze with surprise.

The woodcutters who came into the forest were—as a rule—quiet, observant men who respected the trees and woods as a whole and had learned the trick of the massive misdirection spell that made the forest so easy to get lost in. They came in to gather deadfalls and dropped limbs, working quietly and efficiently, leaving as soon as their task was complete. Braven and his fellows did not harm these men, or even scare them too badly. They did die occasionally, but that was because the woods were dangerous even without Braven's help.

Woodcutters worked alone. The forest had a way of separating those who desired to remain together. So Braven was surprised when he heard not just the voice of one man, but several.

He drifted up behind a tree and pulled his cloak in tight about his body. He closed his eyes and focused, letting his sense of hearing swell and open until he could listen to the conversation of the men several yards away as clearly as if they stood right next to him.

"… knows we're in here," one of them was saying in a low, hesitant tone full of unhappiness.

The voice that answered was the opposite. It rang with confidence and bluster, the unmistakable bravado of some show-off trying to prove something.

"I tell you, it's all fairy stories. When was the last time someone actually died in this woods?"

"Tem Cutter nearly died." These words were spoken by a third voice, short and surly.

There was a thump, as if someone had set a heavy burden down with impatience. "Tem Cutter. Tem Cutter! Why is it he's all anyone ever talks about? Yes, so a snake bit him. He stayed all night beneath the trees. He beat off a pack of dires with his bare hands. If that proves anything, it's that we're all behaving like imbeciles when it comes to this place."

Braven felt his normally sunny mood darken a few notches. He sidled around the tree, straining into the fog, but he could see nothing.

There was no response from the boastful man's companions. Braven considered his options. He had any number of old standby spells he used to spook the woodcutters if they grew too bold. This situation was different, though. These men were here to challenge the forest's mystique. That couldn't be tolerated. He might need to come up with something a little more creative.

"Anyway," the man began again, his voice ringing with hubris. "I've had enough of scraping and scrounging and breaking my back for a pittance. I've had enough of sitting on my hands while there's a fortune in fine timber sitting here for the taking. You two stand back."

Braven felt a prickle at the back of his neck – a warning pulse that something was about to happen. He felt a brief longing for Gia's presence. She was back at the lake. He rarely brought her on his patrol. It was too cool in the forest for her, and she grew uncomfortable out of the water. The bond between them was muted now, made thin by the distance.

A strange sense of urgency making him less cautious than usual, Braven hurried forward, moving on soft feet over the loamy forest floor. He stepped around a final tree just as he heard a loud, sharp, smack and saw a burly, middle-aged man standing with feet planted, shoulders braced, the head of his axe buried up to the shaft in the trunk of one of the sacred trees.

Braven was so shocked, so sickened by the sight, for a moment he could only stare. The man began to work his shoulders, prying the axe head loose. Then he heaved it back again, preparing for another swing.

Rage erupted in Braven in a sudden violent burst. The world seemed to waver as his vision went red at the edges. He felt heat rise to his face. His brain filled with an unfamiliar desire.

He wanted to harm these men.

The man with the axe grunted, reset, and swung again. Again, that horrible sound, the crack of metal biting ancient bark. The man laughed. "See." His voice had a gloating tone. "It's just a blighted tree."

Braven could see the other two men now. They stood a little distance off, shifting uneasily and casting glances into the fog. Though they were only a few trunks past the place where the forest gave way to grass, one of them held a string that stretched back to the wood's edge. They must have tied it off on their way in, so they could find their way back out.

The first man was still talking. "We're going to make our fortune, lads." He pulled the axe free and reset for another strike. It seemed to Braven he was not very handy with the tool. He'd seen other woodcutters chopping their way through deadfalls. They swung with clean, efficient strokes. This man was clumsy.

The thought gave Braven an idea. His rage was a living thing inside him now. He gathered his power, holding it in his mind and bringing it to a focus. Then, he waited.

Everyone always said Braven was talented when it came to casting. He supposed it was because most of what he did was intuitive. He had a feel for the power Gia lent him, and an innate understanding of what could be done with it. While nothing he did felt particularly remarkable to him, many of his peers had to learn their casting spell by painstaking spell.

Braven didn't think. He simply did. The axe rose for a third strike, and Braven sent out a thread of magic on a moving pulse. He watched with grim satisfaction as the muscles beneath the man's shirt flexed. The axe began to fall, its head glinting in the dull light.

The scene seemed to blur. There was a thud, but this time the sound was not as crisp. It was the smack of metal striking flesh rather than bark.

There was a single beat of silence before the man began to scream.

Marim still wasn't easy about the fog. As she reached the end of the garden walk and crossed the gravel yard to the back entrance of Embriem's large house, it annoyed her she couldn't see into the distance. Six months here, and she'd learned the different types of fog, when it was likely to be thick, thin, or restless. She'd made it through the violent storms that came with the changing seasons.

The systems swept across the island and lingered, battering Embriem's house for two or three days sometimes.

After the storms moved on, she'd watched the angle of the light change. As the nights grew slightly cooler and shorter, some trees lost their leaves. Others did not. The hedges and grasses were still green, and there was never any frost or snow. Marim found this strange. It would be the dead of winter in Masidon now, the land frozen and dormant, waiting for spring.

The false winter lent a sort of dreamlike quality to Marim's sense of the passage of time. She felt she had been in this place for ages, and also that she had only just arrived.

And always, there was the fog. It muffled the world every time she set foot outside, making her feel as if she'd lost some sixth sense she'd never previously appreciated.

As she walked, Marim was aware of Kix wheeling above in the damp air. He came to her as she stepped onto the stone stoop and over the threshold, burrowing his small body between her hood and the skin of her throat. She gave a small, gasping laugh. "Kix, you're cold." But she said it fondly, reaching up to run a quick, affectionate finger down his sinuous back.

Her tessila found a comfortable position against her collarbone, and fell still. Marim closed the heavy double doors behind her. They had a tendency to boom if swung quickly, so she guided them shut before turning to make her way up the long hallway that led to the front of the house.

She was about to turn into the entryway and head for the stairs when she heard a door slam. Startled, she turned in time to see Embriem come striding out of his office, holding a letter in his hand. His red tinged hair was sticking out in every direction, his expression dark.

"Baret!" He thundered his butler's name, then noticed Marim standing at the mouth of the hall. Some of the annoyance smoothed out of his face. He modulated his tone, inclining his head in greeting. "Marim. Good day. I didn't see you there. Where's Tassin?"

It was strange, Marim thought, you could live in the same house with a man and see so little of him. Until this moment, she hadn't so much as clapped eyes on Embriem in days. Now, she couldn't help but note certain details about his appearance. He was pale, for one thing, even more so than was normal for the people here. He was still too thin. Unlike his son, Tassin, who had wasted no time packing back on the weight he'd lost during his ordeal, Embriem was not exhibiting much of an appetite. More alarming than all that, though, was the strange, restless glitter in his eyes.

Marim turned to face her employer, resisting the urge to reach up and confirm her collar was high and snug about her throat. "He's with Secha, having his lunch. Mishi will have him changed in time for his piano lesson."

The glitter in Embriem's eyes sparked. Some of the anger came back into his face. He held up the letter and spoke in a disgusted tone. "It would seem Master Flagron no longer cares to be in my employ."

Marim felt a dip of anxiety in her stomach as she stared at the innocuous piece of parchment. She groped for some mollifying statement, some way to put a spin on this latest snub, but her mind was a blank.

Embriem waited, standing next to an oil painting of a ship on the sea in a gilded, ornate frame. His finely made but somewhat rumpled clothing hung loose around the sharp angles of his body. She almost didn't believe her memory of the first time she'd seen him. He'd been so hearty and solid, striding out of the fog with the confidence of a man who is secure in his own place.

When Marim didn't speak, Embriem's shoulders sagged. His eyes drifted to the misty view out the window. "Just as well." His voice was low now, and tired. "His rates are astronomical."

Marim's eyes flickered around the ornate hall. It was dim, even at this peak hour of the day. When she'd first arrived in this house, lamps had been lit in the main living areas all of the time.

Not anymore.

It wasn't any of Marim's business, of course, but it was difficult not to hear the rumors. Though Marim did not go to town often (and when she did, the locals looked at her askance) she overheard gossip nonetheless. Now that Marim was a long-term occupant, Embriem had expanded the household staff by bringing on a live-in housemaid, a nurse to attend Tassin when he wasn't with Marim, and a footman. More than once, Marim had overheard quiet conversations in the back halls. The talk on the island was Embriem's business was struggling.

Marim was grateful to Embriem, but she also knew her own security and stability depended on his. When she'd had nowhere to go, no way to earn her keep, he'd given her a job. Marim was now Tassin's governess. In exchange for teaching his son reading, writing, arithmetic, and basic magics, Embriem provided her food and board, plus a weekly stipend.

It wasn't an outcome Marim had ever expected when she'd first set foot on the deck of the ship that had brought her here. But then, she'd never expected to be dumped off on this strange island either. For the most part, she was grateful to have a roof over her head. Tassin was a sweet child, if a bit disinclined to focus on the non-magical aspects of his education. If Embriem was nothing more in her life than a polite, distant presence, she could hardly complain.

Still, she was concerned for him. She'd learned a lot about the brinlins and their needs since taking over Tassin's care. She couldn't help but prod. "Embriem, when was the last time you went down to the warmlake?"

Embriem stirred, his eyes flicking to her only to slide off again. "Nel's there now." Before she could point out he hadn't answered her question, he seemed to rouse himself. "I'm sorry, Marim. Please excuse me." He strode off towards the back door, once again calling for his butler.

Marim stood looking after him. That would explain the strange glitter in his eyes. She lifted her hand to her neck and ran a finger along Kix's back again. The warmlake was at least two miles away. She and Kix had never been separated by such a distance in all the years since he'd chosen her as his partner. "He's running himself ragged." Marim murmured these words to her tessila as she continued her interrupted journey, up the staircase, down the broad hall, and into her own room. Inside, she closed the door and hung her damp cloak on one of the hooks on the wall.

As was her habit, Marim went first to her desk and removed a slim wooden case from the top drawer. She undid the clasp, feeling the spark of magic in her fingertips as the spell within confirmed her identity. She opened the lid and tipped out the three leather tablets within. They were all identical in size and shape. Two of them had seals stamped into the corner. The first bore the crest of Tessili Academy. The second, Professor Liam's personal chop. The third had no identifying mark.

Marim settled herself into her chair and spread the tablets out in front of her. Two of them, the two with the seals, bore writing. The third did not. As Kix darted off towards the fireplace, Marim read. She took in the words line by line, first from one tablet, then the other. She had picked up her scribis to begin a reply when she noticed something unusual.

The third tablet, the one that bore no seal, suddenly began to change. Words appeared, letter by letter, as someone far away wrote on the tablet linked to this one.

Marim turned from her writing, heart beginning to beat a little faster at the sight of the familiar, slanted hand. She read the words as they formed. "Does Kix socialize with the brinlin?"

This was typical of the tablet's owner. No small talk, no pleasantries, just opaque questions.

Nevertheless, Marim couldn't help herself. She pushed the two other tablets aside and began her answer.

The master suite stood at the back of Embriem's house. When he'd first purchased the building, shortly before he married Chalsia, Embriem remembered being pleased by these chambers the two of them would share. They were spacious, with as expansive a view of the back gardens as the fog would allow. The house, while built in the grand old style, was actually quite new. It came with modern conveniences, like built-in globe lamps that took the distilled oil the traders brought from Masidon. While expensive, the lamps burned pure and bright, not producing any smoke or open flame, and only needing to be refilled a few times a year.

The room, of course, was also equipped with a large fireplace for warmth, but Embriem rarely had it lit these days. What had once been a chamber full of happiness and potential now seemed desiccated and barren. He only allowed himself one lamp now, so the edges of the grand room were always dim. The shadows were a pressure on his mind not dissimilar to his desire to be down by the warmlake, with Nel.

Now, as Embriem undressed in his vast, chilly chamber, he could feel his brinlin's dull sense of loneliness. He had gone to see her that morning. He'd spent nearly half an hour by the warmlake, watching her swim and letting her perch on his fingers. It wasn't enough. He could feel the longing for more time with her in his very bones.

But there were so many other things that needed Embriem's attention. His decision to go public about his new circumstances, he saw now, had been perhaps somewhat hasty. He'd been ready for suspicion and curiosity, maybe a little bit of opposition. He hadn't been prepared for fear. He'd never expected people who'd been his friends all his life to suddenly refuse to acknowledge him in the street. Most of all, he'd not expected others to sever professional ties with him – to refuse to work for him, trade with him, or buy his goods.

In the six months since he and his son had nearly died, Embriem had experienced a slow slide towards insolvency. Each day, it took all of Embriem's effort and energy to shore up his flagging business. He met with people he'd been dealing with for decades, trying to convince them he was the same person he'd always been.

The problem was, no one confronted him directly. No one actually said, straight out, they would not trade with him or would no longer be his friend because he had turned into something they didn't understand – a human who'd formed a magical bond with a brinlin. Instead, people shifted away from him. They canceled meetings or failed to follow through on verbal agreements. There was always a vague explanation. Less revenue. A modified trade route. A new supplier.

But it always came back to the same reality. Embriem's finances were on the verge of disaster.

Now, as he pulled off his shirt and tossed it onto an overstuffed chair, he caught the glint of reflected light in the mirror affixed to the far wall. He could remember Chalsia, the way she used to stand here and grimace at herself when she was pregnant, noting her puffy face, the bags under her eyes. He remembered seeing only beauty where she saw imperfection. He would put his hands on her smooth skin, kiss her neck, tell her how he loved her changing body.

As always, thoughts of Chalsia brought the darkness up in him. It rose in his sternum like a sea monster, heavy and coiling, to tear at his heart. The problem was, he still couldn't believe, even all these years later, that Chalsia was dead. He couldn't imagine a life without her. Instead, Embriem felt he was waiting. He was waiting, and his wonderful wife, his best friend, would someday reward his patience by coming home. She would waltz through the front door and hand off her cloak as if she'd just been down in the town doing some shopping.

It was mad to think that way, Embriem knew. He turned away from the mirror, slipped off his trousers, and made his way towards the hulking shape of the bed. He was about to climb between the sheets when the door to his chamber flew open with a bang.

Embriem wheeled, his heart suddenly gripped with terror and understanding alike. They had come at last. The people of Lan Dinas, no longer content to merely stonewall him, had risen up against him in earnest. He cast about the room for a weapon, taking one stride towards where his belt knife sat atop a nearby chair.

Then he heard the patter of bare feet on tile. Tassin ran towards his father, wearing his night clothes and jabbering in his high, excited voice.

It took Embriem a moment to parse the reality of what was happening. It was not an attack, only his son – awake for some reason at this ungodly hour, and somehow snuck away from his own rooms.

Slowly, Tassin's words began to penetrate through the alarm in Embriem's mind. "… worked at it all day but couldn't figure it out. But now, because I couldn't sleep, I was practicing and I got it, Da. I figured it out. Look."

Tassin had stopped a little way into the room. He stood now, looking at his father with an expression of excitement. He had his mother's complexion, eyelashes of pale gold, fine, bright hair.

As Embriem watched, his son's little brows pulled together. He assumed a look of exaggerated concentration, held up his hand, palm open, and stood in utter stillness.

One moment passed, then another. Embriem's alarm was fading to annoyance. Where was the nurse? It was her job to make sure Tassin was put to bed properly. How had the boy made it all the way down the stairs and across the house unnoticed?

He was about to walk across the room and pull his trousers on, about the take his son firmly by the wrist and escort him back to his own chambers, when he saw the light.

It was the teeniest of sparks at first, nothing more than the hint of bobbing luminance above his son's palm. He caught his breath, blinked, and looked again.

Tassin's face was the picture of concentration. He took in a deep breath, compressed his lips, and suddenly a glowing sphere leapt into being, suspended above his small palm.

Embriem stared at his son with a combined sensation of fear and wonder. He himself had not had any time to spare for learning about the magics he could now theoretically wield, but he'd asked Marim to teach Tassin. And Tassin was, apparently, learning.

The blackness turned over in Embriem chest again. Chalsia, he thought bitterly, would never see this. She would never see their son balance a glowing orb on his palm.

The thought drained him of warmth. He felt an urge to speak harshly, to snap at Tassin for leaving his bedroom when he should have been sleeping.

There was a movement in the doorway. Embriem glanced up to see a shape in the hall – the outline of a woman's form.

Although it was impossible, Embriem felt suddenly certain it was Chalsia, home at last.

Then he took in certain details. The woman's hair was too short, her shoulders too square.

It was Marim, not his dead wife. The Tessilari stood staring into the gloom of the bedroom wrapped in her housecoat, spiked hair askew.

As Embriem watched, he saw Marim take in the scene. She saw him notice her, and she spoke in a small voice. "I'm sorry. I felt the spell. I thought something was wrong. I'll go now."

As Marim melted back into the shadows, Embriem felt as if his heart would burst with disappointment and sorrow. Even as he looked back at his son, who was holding the glowing globe and looking at his father with hopeful eyes, Embriem realized something else.

His wife would have been thrilled for Tassin, fascinated by Nel and Tibs. She would never have spent all her time worrying about money when there was magic to be learned.

The room where Marim gave Tassin his lessons was on the second floor, attached to the boy's bedroom and playroom. It was a large, airy space, one wall lined in bookshelves, with various desks and surfaces placed strategically along walls or in corners. There were cozy chairs for reading, a sloped desk for drawing and painting, and a long, flat table for crafts, activities, and experiments. It struck Marim as an excessive amount of space for a six-year-old boy to fill.

And that was just the schoolroom. It was attached to a play area that housed toys and games, which in turn attached to the bedroom where an elaborate four-poster stood in massive splendor. Attached to that was another bedroom that was now occupied by the nurse, whose primary duty was to get Tassin up in the morning, get him dressed, keep his chambers tidy, see he ate his meals, put him to bed at night, and make sure he stayed in bed once put there.

She'd failed at that last duty only the night before. Now, as Tassin sat at his desk, swinging his legs and grimacing down at the pencil he was trying to move with a tiny little active push spell, Marim couldn't help but think back on the strange moment she'd witnessed from the hall outside Embriem's room. She'd seen Tassin, so small and slight in his pale pajamas, standing in his father's vast, shadowy bedroom with a little passive luminance spell balanced on his palm.

While that had been remarkable in its own right, what had really surprised Marim was Embriem's face. He hadn't seemed proud or delighted or awed at his son's accomplishment.

He'd seemed enraged.

Now, as Kix fluttered around the high ceiling, exploring the deep relief patterns in the crown molding, Marim tried to understand. She could believe Embriem might have been annoyed at Tassin for leaving his bed. Still, it was hardly a crime for a young, lonely child who had just experienced a huge change in his life to seek comfort or company. How many nights, long ago, had Coll come sneaking through the darkened pathways of the academy in the warm night, his boyish face streaked with tears? How many times had she dried those tears, held him, done what she could to calm him, and led him back to bed with no one the wiser?

Tassin now was a year younger than Coll had been when he'd first arrived at the academy. Marim had been an initiate then, only seven or eight years older than her charges, but already helping with the pre-initiates and serving the roll she would continue to occupy even after her own graduation. Coll, that thin, sad-eyed boy had seen something sympathetic in her. Ever after, he always came to her when he was upset, lonely, scared, or confused.

Watching Tassin, Marim felt a brief stab of homesickness. The ship that could take her home would not return for at least six months more. After the dramatic events that had led to Tassin and Embriem bonding with their brinlins, Marim had thought she'd found a place here – somewhere to belong.

In the months that had passed since then, Marim had been disappointed to find Embriem more distant and preoccupied with each passing day. Now, after seeing his face last night, she wasn't so sure she wanted to stay here much longer.

Tassin, she noticed, was not focused on his spell. He was craned around in his chair, staring towards the window. His desk was positioned deliberately away from any windows that might provide distraction. It wasn't that he was high spirited or overly energetic. He was a quiet, compliant child. He was diligent when it came to learning the weave of passive spells, but active ones seemed to confound him. It didn't make sense. In Marim's experience, active spells, being less subtle, were easier for young casters to learn.

Sighing, Marim rose, trying to think of some way to motivate him. He wasn't unintelligent. On the contrary, he was quick to pick up on most concepts. He also wasn't incapable. With a little effort, he could accomplish the majority of the tasks she set before him.

He just couldn't get a handle on active casting.

With passive magic, it was another matter. He was endlessly fascinated, motivated to experiment and learn.

She was about to go to him, to explain again that magic required balance. Passive spells were important, but one could not develop a complete understanding of weave theory without spending time studying both methodologies.

So far, her encouragement was in vain. Still, she rose from her armchair and was about to cross the room when she saw Embriem.

He was standing outside the doorway, partly hidden by the frame. From his position, he had a vantage to see his son. His posture seemed to indicate he'd been there for a while.

When Marim moved, his eyes flicked to her. And there was that strange glitter in them again. *Embriem*, she thought. *You are playing with fire.*

Like with Tassin, she couldn't seem to influence Embriem's behavior with logic. It was accepted among the Tessilari that tessili and their bound partners needed to stay near each other most of the time. Too much separation led to madness. This was a well-documented fact. She had explained this to Embriem over and over, citing sources, explaining risks. And yet, day after day, Embriem left Nel in the warmlake, going to her only for brief visits.

It wasn't enough.

At the sight of Embriem, Marim felt a shiver of unease. Was she living with a man who was in the process of coming unhinged?

But when her employer spoke, his voice sounded normal enough. "Marim. A word?" Without waiting for a reply, he withdrew.

Marim told Tassin he could take a break and work on his passive luminance spell, then followed Embriem into the hall.

He was waiting on the landing, wearing a loose shirt and plain trousers. He turned when she approached. She remembered the way he'd looked last night: bare-chested and enraged. What if that anger erupted again, this time finding a target in her?

She needn't have worried. There was no anger in Embriem today. In the light of the hall, he looked tired, his shoulders thin and sharp. He let out a short sigh as she stopped next to him and said without any kind of preamble, "I think I must ask you to become my governess as well."

Marim stared at him, shocked. A strange, sad smile flickered across his face. He wasn't looking at her. Rather, he was gazing at the portrait of a young woman that hung on the wall. She was pale, with golden eyelashes and a full, smiling mouth. Marim had seen the painting many times. It was Chalsia. Tassin's deceased mother, Embriem's lost wife.

When Marim said nothing, Embriem's eyes shifted away from the painting. He looked directly at Marim with an expression of weary resolve. "If the entire town is going to punish me for my magical abilities, I might as well learn a few spells."

The first time Cockram had been invited into the rector's office, he'd been a boy of only nine years old. He could still remember how the room had seemed to him that first time. Attached to the front of the rector's living quarters, the office was built in the same elevated, ornate style as the cloister, the church, and the three naves. The door was heavy and thick. When pushed, it swung ponderously inwards on its well-oiled hinges. The windows were narrow and tall, pointed at the tops, with patterns and figures carved into the sills and supports. Cockram had been awed by both the room and the man who sat behind the large desk and spoke to him.

That was a long time ago now. Some thirty years had passed since the death of Cockram's sister. The rector, whose hair had been unusually dark when he arrived from Elys Yins to take up his position, had faded to white in the intervening years. His skin had sagged and loosened. So, apparently, had his will.

Back then, Cockram had been the uncertain one, the one who needed guidance and support. Now, it appeared the tables had turned.

It seemed Cockram had made a hundred visits to this room since the events that had unfolded six months ago, when a single day had changed everything. Embriem's son should have died – should have been released from his suffering and guided across Tristis' threshold. Instead, Embriem and his son both had made bonds of magic with the monsters that lived in the lake. In doing so, they'd shaken the fundamental beliefs that governed life on this island. Also, Cockram had lost an eye.

And yet, the rector had done nothing. No action against the abomination that had arisen in their very midst had been so much as suggested, never mind undertaken. Although Cockram had pushed and prodded, even offered suggestions and support, the rector had not acted. Both Tassin and Embriem had at least two marks against them. They should be tested with the ring or the rod and destroyed before the corruption spread. It was all there, spelled out in the Directive. Beyond that, there was the not insignificant matter of the Tessilari who had used her dark power to stay the church's hand when Tassin might have been released from his suffering.

To Cockram, these events were a direct assault on everything the Directive stood for. To Cockram, it looked like the beginning of the cascade effect the document had been created to prevent.

And yet, Dinon had not acted. He was shaken by the discovery that brinlins and tessili appeared to share similar qualities. He was uncertain if the Vaulted Fathers on Elys Yins knew of this connection. He was unwilling to act without explicit instructions from his superiors.

He was, in short, experiencing a crisis of faith.

Now, as Dinon entered his office through the doors in the back, looking wan and a little sunken in his heavy red robes, Cockram turned and regarded him with his one remaining eye, absently adjusting the golden rooster pin in his neck scarf. Wearily, Dinon settled behind his desk, groped for a key he wore about his neck, unhooked it from its chain, and tossed it onto the desk.

Cockram stared at the key. He knew what it opened. The locked box was hidden behind a panel in the wall. Inside rested the sacred manuscript Cockram had devoted his life to upholding. Always before, Dinon had opened the box if it needed to be opened. Now, there was something sour and weary in the rector's face as he said, "I've heard from the Vaulted Fathers. Open the box if you wish."

Anticipation, hot and sharp, surged through Cockram. His hand shook a little as he reached for the key, so he snatched it up quickly and turned to the wall. He worked the secret panel with ease, having watched Dinon do it a hundred times. The panel slid aside, the box appeared, shallow but wide. He lifted it from its hiding place and carried it to the desk, where he used the key to undo the ornate golden lock on the front.

Inside lay the Directive, written in a vaulted hand, the letters well-formed and flowery. On top lay a face down piece of parchment that seemed to have been tossed carelessly into the box. Cockram picked it up and turned it over.

The response was brief – brusque even. Cockram read the words as another thrilling rush of adrenaline shot through his body. "The Directive is absolute. Do not waver, Dinon. It is your sworn duty to measure every soul you meet by its standards, and deliver release to the corrupted."

Cockram raised his eyes. Dinon was watching him, his face blank and tired. He spoke without invitation, certain their rolls had shifted at last. Long ago, it was Cockram who had doubted and hedged and hesitated. Now, it was his turn to lead.

"I have a plan."

Dinon gave a small nod. Cockram told him what they would do. When he was done, the rector sighed, rubbing his face with his hands. His voice was subdued when he spoke, but he did not argue. "It will work if Delari's will is with us."

In the box, next to the Directive itself, lay a blunt, silver wand. Cockram had seen it before. It was one of two items that could be used in the final test. It could take the measure of a person with two marks already against him, and decide his fate.

Dinon saw him eyeing the artifact, and spoke. "Take it, my son. You might need to wield it against the Tessilari."

With a surge of excitement, Cockram reached for the rod. As his fingers brushed the cool metal, he felt a dull shock in his sternum, as if he'd been stabbed with a short, brutal knife. There was a flash of pain. He went briefly woozy, and he smelled the scent of singed fabric.

His eye blinked, his vision cleared, and he forced himself to pick up the rod as if nothing had happened. Dinon was watching him with unnerving intensity, so he slid the artifact quickly into his pocket. He said, "I'll let you know when it is time."

Before Dinon could notice the pin in his scarf had grown so hot it was burning the fabric, Cockram turned and strode out of the rectory.

CHAPTER 2

Adni heard the door to the rector's office swing open. She pulled her hood a little higher, though she was well cloaked in shadow. As Cockram walked out the door, she released the passive reach spell that had allowed her to hear the conversation he'd been having with the rector. He marched away into the fog, and Adni resisted the urge to follow.

It was too dangerous to go after him. She was already taking more risks than she should, coming this close to the town before sundown. But she had faith in the magic of her cloak. She'd woven it herself, infusing the fabric with a strong passive echo spell that would make a person who saw her fail to register her presence unless she did something impossible to ignore, like speak to him or touch him. It had allowed her to see without being seen many times.

Sneaking around was one of Adni's specialties.

Many people didn't consider her skillset to be desirable, yet few hesitated to employ her to undertake the actions they preferred not to deal with themselves. Over the years, Adni's reputation for discretion and competence (a rare and valuable combination) meant she could pick and choose the jobs she accepted and still have all the work she cared to take.

Now, watching Cockram's back recede into the fog, she was aware her task was complete. She'd gained the information she'd been sent to collect. She should go back now, slip down to the lakeshore and unmoor the slender canoe she'd left hidden among the reeds. She should paddle back up the lake to where it narrowed, became a river, and entered the ancient wood. She should row up that river until it broadened into a lake again, and tie her craft up to the delicate, heartwood pier outside her house. She should report what she'd learned to the Wheel, and return home for a meal and some rest.

But that wasn't what she wanted to do.

Adni was used to this conflict between desire and duty. It had been present in her life since her earliest memories, starting with her ferocious childhood desire to spend as much time by the warmlake as possible in spite of her parents' admonition never to go there.

Now, feeling the familiar urge to go after Cockram, to stalk him, to follow him back to his dreary pub and watch him go about the mundane tasks of his daily life, Adni was rescued from the thrall of temptation by the ring of voices in the fog. She melted back to stand against the wall.

A moment later, a man materialized out of the mist. He was running, gasping for breath, and he was red. His face was red with exertion. His hands were red also, his clothing stained a dark crimson going brown as it dried.

Blood, Adni realized with an unpleasant shock. This man was covered in blood.

As she watched from the shadows, the man hurried to the rector's door and raised a fist to pound on the heavy wood.

It took only a moment for Dinon to answer. From her vantage against the wall, Adni could not see the rector, but she heard the visitor's wild words clearly enough. "Please, come quickly. It's Billit. He was …" Here the man paused oddly, his words cut off as if he'd caught himself about to say something verboten. He recovered and went on, the words tumbling out in a jumble. "He got hurt by an axe, whacked himself right in the leg. We were there, me and Mart. We saw it. It was the strangest thing. The axe slipped and we carried him all the way here but he's all over blood and gone so pale and cold."

The rector, face serious, was already moving. He stepped out his door and strode into the fog, walking with long, efficient strides towards the infirmary. Too interested to leave now, Adni followed.

As they walked, the man nattered on, rubbing his bloody hands on his bloody tunic. "Cockram came upon us, which was a godsend because I'm so tired, like, I could hardly keep my grip any longer. He took my place and told me to come get you."

Adni knew the only role the rector would have in the infirmary was the delivery of the final blessing: the preparation of a soul for death. If Cockram had told this man to come get Dinon, he must have believed there was small hope for the injured man's survival.

The two men walked quickly, Adni moving in their wake, the fog shifting and coiling around her. The cloister grounds were well-groomed and open. Adni took the calculated risk of walking a short way behind the two men. The fog was not particularly thick today, so she was in plain view. But she believed her cloak would do its job.

They overtook the others on the path to the cloister. Cockram stood on the path, bristling with impatience, while a second figure stood nearby, doubled over, hands on knees. He was a stout man with a face even more flushed than his companion's, and blood soaked into the sleeves of his shirt.

The third man lay on the ground, and Adni felt what the rector saw instantaneously. As Dinon's somber voice sounded in the fog, she withdrew a few steps.

Whatever happened, Cockram could not see her. No passive echo spell in the world would be strong enough to blot out the shock the sight of her would give him.

"There is no need to take him to the infirmary." Dinon's words were full of sad resignation. "This man has already crossed Tristis' threshold."

A silence fell over the group. The wound was in the man's thigh, high on the leg. It had been clumsily bound in the man's own shirt, so Adni couldn't see how large it might be. Nevertheless, there was something about the position of the bandage that did not ring true with the story she'd heard.

The rector, kneeling to take the man's pulse for confirmation of what was already obvious, saw it too. He straightened, folded his hands within his sleeves, and looked at the two blood-stained men. "You say he hit himself?"

Both men nodded, but neither spoke. They stood, one on either side of their fallen companion, both drooping with exhaustion.

Dinon waited a beat. When neither man offered any further information, the rector went on. "I don't see how he could have accomplished that, given the wound's position. If I didn't know better, I would think someone else had done the swinging."

A strange, low whine began to escape from the throat of the thin man who had run to rector's office. The stout man, Mart, turned to look at his companion, an expression of alarm on his face. "Todi." He spoke urgently. "We agreed."

But Todi appeared unable to contain himself. His words came out in a tumble, full of pain and confusion. He turned to the rector, extending a blood-stained hand towards the holy man as he began to speak. "We were in the woods, a little ways in is all. Billit had got it in his head he was going to cut down a tree. One of the big ones, healthy and living. He never told us that until we were there. We never knew what he meant to do. All he said was we should go with him and we'd make our fortune. I was curious, like, so I did go but I was uneasy when I saw where he meant to take us. I was about to go back on my own, to leave him to his plans, when he started chopping. He was swinging his axe and whacking away at one of the huge trunks. We didn't know what to do. Me and Mart here, we were stunned. Billit kept swinging, going on about the price of timber and how we'd be so rich. Then, sudden like, the axe was in his leg instead of the tree. It wasn't me or Mart, I swear on the three Vaulted Gods and Vestima's crime. It was the evil forest's magic made this happen."

Adni saw surprise and horror flicker across the rector's face as the story spilled out. She felt a shock herself: a thrum of unease in her chest.

She took a few steps backwards, then turned to hurry away.

It was time for her to go home.

✛

When she'd been a child in the valley of Deramor, Marim had never seen a tessila. Back then, there had been no brillbane in the forest or along the river, and so neither had there been any tessili. Together, the two species, plant and animal, had been entirely eradicated from the wild.

In the years since the return of the Tessilari, brillbane seeds had been scattered in plenty. Restored to their native environment, the wild tessila population had begun to spread beyond the academy walls. But according to the histories, the banks of the river that ran by Deramor had once been thick with brillbane and tessili alike. Marim knew this, knew tessili once existed the way brinlins did now.

Still, she could never quite get used to the warmlake. The sheer number of brinlins in the water, the massive scale of the population that lived among the reeds, boggled her mind. Stranger still, it was as if the magic of the brinlins had seeped into the land somehow, imbuing the soil and vegetation and sky with enchantment. The reeds, for instance, grew in abundance. Tassin explained how they always grew back overnight, no matter how many were chopped down and hauled off during the day. Marim, not believing him, cut a few stalks with her belt-knife one afternoon. When they returned the following morning, she found the reeds undamaged.

Still, she didn't believe. She thought she'd made a mistake. There were, after all, many, many reeds along the shore. She conducted her experiment again, this time marking the stubs of the reeds she cut with ribbons.

In the morning, she discovered the impossible. Her ribbons were there—a bit bedraggled with the damp—but the reeds they were tied to were as tall and whole as any others.

The phenomenon confounded her. There was no provision for this in what she'd learned at the academy. Magic, she'd been taught, was inert unless tapped by a human.

Except here on Cynnes Tarth, apparently.

One fine morning several weeks after Embriem had asked her to teach him magic, Marim, Tassin, and Embriem all stood together on one of the spits of sand where the reeds did not grow. Marim had persuaded Embriem to leave his house with some difficulty. Now he stood with an impatient air, gazing off into the fog.

So far, her efforts at teaching Embriem about magics hadn't amounted to much. For one thing, he was constantly cutting their lessons short in favor of business obligations. For another, he was not as intuitive as his son. So far, they hadn't even approached the point where he could learn a spell. She'd put him to the remedial task of simply pulling threads for use in his weaves, working on learning to be consistent in length and width. But he didn't apply himself to these exercises, seeming to find them demeaning.

Working with Embriem brought back painful memories of Marim's own remedial lessons at the academy. Watching him struggle with his threads, Marim came to believe his issue wasn't in his own capacity, but in his bond with Nel. He'd been too much apart from her for too long.

So, she'd suggested this field trip. As the three of them listened to the shush and sigh of the water and the reeds, Marim rattled on about the theory of magics. "Spells may be passive or active. Passive spells are less potent but less tiring, and can be held for periods of time. Active spells are usually one-offs. You cast them all in a moment and release them into the world."

She couldn't tell if Embriem was listening or not. Tassin already knew this lesson. It was proving to be a little awkward, teaching both of them. Embriem was much quicker to grasp complex concepts than his young son, but had a tendency to ask questions Marim found herself incapable of answering. The previous afternoon, she'd gotten started by explaining how the bond between a tessila or brinlin and its human was a linking of their life force. If one died, the other would as well. As she'd said this, Embriem had narrowed his eyes and asked why.

Marim hadn't known what to say. She wasn't Delari, after all. She hadn't woven the world out of moonbeams before setting all the animals on its surface. She wasn't even Vestima, the rebellious younger goddess who had spilled magic into the earth. But she was a little irritated with Embriem for making her task of teaching him so hard. So she'd scowled right back. "What do you mean, why?"

Embriem made a gesture of impatience. "It doesn't make any sense. How could Nel's death affect me? She's so small – not a fraction of my size."

Marim had tried to explain. "Size makes no difference. A large animal is no more alive than a small one. Your life is hers now, and hers is yours. It is one life you share. Two lives, become one."

Embriem's face had suggested he was not satisfied, but he hadn't pressed the point. Now, as she explained about passive and active spells, she braced herself for more questions. But Embriem was standing with Nel perched on his finger. That strange glitter had left his eyes for the moment. He seemed more relaxed than she'd seen him in weeks. Tassin wasn't paying the least bit of attention to her lecture. He was kneeling on the shore, giggling as he and Tibs played some incomprehensible game.

Marim, feeling stymied, stopped talking. She watched her two distracted charges with a feeling of annoyance. How was she supposed to teach them if they didn't listen?

But Embriem turned his head after she'd been silent for a moment. "Which is easier?"

The fog was thin today, the sun pouring into it from above. Embriem's eyes were brilliant in his pale face, a luminous, pale blue. Marim found herself suddenly flustered. Kix, who'd been climbing around on the reeds trying to sneak up on a brinlin, flew to her and alighted on her shoulder, treating Embriem to a hard stare. "Easier?"

Nel ran up Embriem's hand to sit on his shoulder. The brinlin's hide, Marim realized, was almost the exact sky blue shade as Embriem's eyes.

Embriem's look became a little incredulous. He repeated his question. "Passive or active spells. Which is easier?"

Marim felt a spark of annoyance. It was the wrong question. The two kinds of casting were different. It wasn't possible to compare them, to hold one up against the other this way.

She was about to attempt to explain this when Kix suddenly sat up straight on her shoulder and held himself at quivering attention. Then he lit into the air, straight as an arrow, and flew away into the fog.

Marim stood for a moment, staring after him. The cursed fog made it impossible to see where he'd gone. In a fit of annoyance and inspiration, she cast a spell.

She didn't have a name for it. It wasn't one she'd learned at the academy. It was an idea that came to her out of nowhere. She simply pulled her threads and wove her spell, brow furrowed in concentration.

She released the spell, and waited. There was no sound or movement but the rattling reeds, no change in the warm, heavy air. Marim felt a dip of disappointment, thinking she'd failed.

Then, the fog began to move. Sluggishly at first, then with more momentum, it rolled away from Marim as if pushed by a storm front. It tumbled and writhed, drawing further and further back from the little spit of sand where she stood.

As the fog receded, the glassy surface of the lake came into view. A lone canoe appeared in the distance, moving across the water at a slow but steady rate. As Marim stared in confusion, she thought for a moment it was empty – that the oars were somehow pulling of their own accord.

She narrowed her eyes, staring, and felt the strange dip in her mind that meant she'd seen through a spell.

Blinking, her head light with sudden fatigue, Marim had only an instant stare before the fog returned, rolling back to swallow her view.

The canoe had been manned by a single figure in a cloak, paddling with smooth, efficient strokes up the lake towards a distant shore lined in towering trees.

The fog collapsed back around Marim. She felt a momentary chill. The air was always warm here on the shore, but it was also thick and clinging. She turned to Embriem, who was looking at her with an expression of mild confusion. "Did you do that? With the fog, I mean?"

Marim blinked a few times, feeling woozy. Kix swept back to her, materializing out of the fog to alight on her shoulder. He strutted a little, proud of himself. Marim felt herself steady, his high spirits buoying her.

She gestured towards the lake. "Did you see it? The canoe? The person inside was using a passive echo spell."

Embriem turned to look out into the fog, though obviously it was much too late to see anything. Nel crawled into his collar in search of a warm place against his neck, only her dangling tail giving away her presence. "That's magic of some sort? But how is that possible? No one else on this island knows any." His tone was doubtful.

Marim felt her mouth tighten. When she'd been younger and insecure about her stunted powers, she'd used to lie about spells she'd cast, trying to impress the other students with false tales of her own accomplishments. They hadn't believed her. They'd looked at her much the way Embriem was looking at her now, with hooded skepticism and sometimes pity.

She resisted the urge to say something snappish. Turning her back on Embriem, she stared into the thin fog. The surface of the lake threw back the weak sunlight. The small waves lapped against the shore, sparkling and sighing. Tassin, crouched on the shore, giggled as his brinlin leapt off his hand into the clear water. He looked up, his eyes alight, and said in an offhand tone. "It could have been Vailria."

Vailria.

The name shot through Marim like a bolt of raw power. She gasped as her mind bucked and bent. Magic that had been hastily patched over her memories of the terrible day Tassin had almost died burned away like dew in the noonday sun. The woozy feeling came back tenfold. She would have fallen had Embriem not reached out and caught her arm. Kix hissed, but Embriem only said, "Oh, quiet down you," as he helped Marim lower herself into a sitting position on the sand.

Vailria.

The name echoed and boomed in Marim's mind, filling her with a raw sense of horror. She remembered that afternoon now, the final confrontation. She'd come into Embriem's sitting room to find him nearly bewitched, ready to follow that woman away somewhere, to leave Lan Dinas and Marim behind.

Nausea swept over her. She doubled over, certain she'd be sick. How could she have forgotten Vailria? She remembered their argument, the shield she'd held over Embriem and herself. Vailria beginning to walk away. Marim had let her guard down and experienced a short-lived moment of horror and realization as she felt a spell take hold of her.

Then, nothing. She could not remember what had happened after that, only waking the next morning in her own bed. She'd not thought of Vailria once in all the time between then and this terrible moment.

Mind magic was difficult. It required power, determination, practice and, most importantly, touch. Marim had never heard of a Tessilari who could have affected the mind from halfway across the room.

But Vailria's had done it, somehow. Her spell had settled on Marim's mind and lain there like a net, separating all her memories of Vailria from the rest of Marim's thoughts.

Fortunately, mind magic was fragile. Pulled on the wrong way, it would simple dissolve. Marim's head was clearing, the confusion swept aside by a rising tide of anger. She looked up at Embriem, who towered over her, his sharp shoulders a screen between her and the muted sun. "Where is Vailria? We haven't seen her since that night."

Embriem frowned. "Vailria." He repeated the name under his breath the way one might speak of a distant childhood friend not thought of in years. "I don't remember Vailria." His tone was bemused.

She could have been gentler, but the old rage was rising in Marim. She felt the familiar helplessness, the sense of being too weak, too unskilled, always one step behind.

She reached up and snatched Embriem's hand, drawing on her bond with Kix. She still wasn't entirely accustomed to the new depth of his power, and pulled a bit more than she needed.

Spells to dispel other spells were some of the easiest active casting, more to do with brute force than subtlety or craft. Marim groped at Embriem, found the dangling residue of Vailria's magic in him, and blasted at it with an active dispel spell.

The magic shattered, falling away from Embriem in brilliant shards. His hand clenched in Marim's, then released. With a gasp, he collapsed onto his knees next to her, dragged himself forward, and vomited into the warmlake.

Marim watched him, her anger fading into fatigue. "Sorry," she said.

Embriem said nothing for a time. He knelt where he was, his back to her, his shoulders heaving. After a few minutes, he reached down and cupped some water into his hands, and splashed his face.

Tassin, eyes wide with confusion, looked from Marim to his father and back again. "Da?" His tone was hesitant, worried.

Embriem shook his head as if to clear it, then pushed himself to his feet. Turning, he looked down at Marim, his eyes sparking with some emotion she could not identify. "Vailria." He spoke the name with certainty now. "She came to me that day, before you came down from your room. She tried to convince me to flee with her into the forest."

Marim blinked, turning to look up the shore of the warmlake. The thick stands of reeds ran on in both directions, seeming endless. "Forest," she said. "What forest?"

Embriem stood staring out over the warmlake, but he didn't see the water or the fog or the reeds. He didn't see the wan sunlight or the white sand or Marim standing next to him. He saw instead the towering trunks of ancient trees, the brilliant shapes of the green ferns.

What forest? Marim's question brought a swell of memories that broke over him like a storm front. All of a sudden, he remembered the forest. And his memories were not from the perspective of one outside looking in, of a boy standing on the safe vantage of the hillside where he'd often strayed when he should have been watching his family's herd of goras. No. He remembered the woods from the inside. He remembered walking among the great trunks, past them. He remembered Chalsia's voice. *You must hunt the edge to find the heart.*

Shuddering, his mind scrambling to reconcile this new truth with the one he'd always believed, Embriem felt his eyes grow hot.

His gut clenched again, but he forced himself to draw in a deep breath and remain steady.

Vailria.

How could he have forgotten? She'd always been there, wearing her dress with its strange, high collar, always at the edge of his life, watching. He remembered her outside the woods that day, the day he'd led Tem Cutter to safety. He remembered her setting her hand on his.

He blinked to clear his head. "Vailria steals memories." His voice came out rough and a little unsteady. "She made me forget I went into the woods with Chalsia, that I found her father. I saved him. Why would she do that?"

Marim was staring off into the fog, her expression speculative. "I expect she's protecting something. Tell me, Embriem, is this forest of yours haunted? Does it have a way of turning you around, so you go in walking straight forward only to find yourself at the edge of it again?"

The fog, thin already, stirred in a light breeze and grew ragged. The reeds rattled. Brinlins leapt into the water, releasing their thin, wild cries. Embriem stared at Marim, his mind too jumbled to understand. "A little bit. Not exactly. But it is awfully easy to get lost in there. It separates people, confuses them. How did you know?"

Marim sighed, fidgeting with her collar. "There's another place much the same. It turns away people who try to find it. It's called the Valley of Mist, and it's where the Tessilari hid for centuries after the people of Masidon turned against them."

Embriem had never been much interested in history. He knew only the sketchiest outline of the events that had surrounded the fall of the magical peoples on the distant mainland. Now, though, his mind seemed to sharpen, aligning facts and evidence, a picture slowly coming together.

He looked at Marim. In her eyes, he could see the same understanding beginning to form. She was the one who put it into words. "You and Tassin are not anomalies, like we thought. There must be a whole hidden population here, just like in Masidon. They must live in the forest and use their magic to keep non-magical people out. That's where Vailria tried to take you – to your people. Whoever they are."

Embriem, listening to Marim, didn't miss the bitter twist in her words as she fell silent. He didn't overlook the way she wrapped her arms around her torso, drawing inward as she spoke. He had often wondered about Marim's history, the past that had driven her from her home. She tried to hide the scars on her neck, but he'd seen them. Now, for the first time, he wondered why she'd been so eager to throw in her lot with utter strangers.

"What happened to your neck?" The question was out of him, past his lips and hanging on the air before Embriem had even decided to speak.

Marim went still. She was standing with her cloak pulled in tight, though the heavy air was warm. She didn't look at him. She'd gone stony and silent.

Tassin broke in, excited and distracted, his high voice piping up with eager curiosity. "How do we find them? Vailria, and the other people like us?"

Marim, turning, gave Tassin a sad sort of smile. "We go to the forest, of course."

Embriem watched her for a moment. She turned to meet his gaze, a sort of challenge shining in her eyes.

Tassin looked up as well, his face full of curiosity. "Can we go really, Da? Into the forest? Isn't it dangerous?"

Embriem answered Tassin, his eyes still on Marim. "It is dangerous, Tassin. Too dangerous." Then, as Marim opened her mouth to protest, he cut her off. "No, Marim. I'm not leading my child off on some mad witch hunt just because you saw a boat on the warmlake." He felt suddenly, inexplicably angry with her. He stood a moment, chest heaving. The frustration he'd been feeling at not being able to manage even basic spells mounted into misdirected anger. Combined with the confusion brought on by the returned memories Marim had just unlocked in his mind, Embriem felt his grip on his patience slip and give way.

Abruptly, it was all too much. He reached down and hauled Tassin to his feet, ignoring his son's protests. "Enough. This is a waste of time. Tassin, you have practical things to learn, like reading and writing. And I've got work to do."

The door to the Rooster's Comb banged open, admitting a group of dock workers. Jostling and laughing, the young men crowded into the common room and slammed the door behind them. They made for a table, heavy boots clomping across the papery reeds strewn on the floor. As Tilde made her way across the dim room to take their order, Cockram stood behind the bar and glowered. Ever since he'd lost the eye, he'd been sensitive to sound. He'd never before noticed how many men crashed their way through the world as if their sense of self-worth hinged on making as much noise as possible.

The dock workers settled into chair seats, joking with Tilde and shrugging out of their heavy coats. Only a few tables were occupied, early as it was. Still, Cockram found himself pouring drinks and wiping down the counter while impatience seethed beneath his skin, only to look up with too much interest each time the door opened.

Tilde left the table, tossing some comment back over her shoulder to make the dock workers laugh. She strode up to the other side of the bar and opened her mouth, about to tell her father what to pour. But something in his face gave her pause. She shut her mouth again and stepped around the bar to fill the order herself.

Cockram watched her pull four tankards out from beneath the bar. She'd matured since he'd been injured, stepping up without protest to take up the slack as he recovered. She was growing easier with the customers, beginning to display some of her mother's gift for handling men. It was useful, this newfound maturity of hers. But it came with a price. He would turn sometimes and catch her out of the corner of his eye. He'd feel a bolt of shock, a moment of recognition, thinking it was not his daughter who stood there, but his wife.

Each time it happened, Cockram had to take himself out of the Rooster's Comb for a time. He couldn't walk like he'd used to walk. His calf still pained him, and his head would begin to throb before he'd gone a mile. So he would haul himself off into the fog and sit, seething with hateful memories, until he could divert his mind back to more useful topics. Topics like his plan.

Cockram's plan was in his mind every moment he was awake. True, he had, suffered a setback. But he was not defeated. The Tessilari girl might think she'd won. She certainly went about town openly enough, walking down to the warmlake every day with the corrupted child in tow. The few times he'd seen her, she'd seemed unafraid, certain, and confident.

Which was all to the good. She would be easier to take down if she wasn't on her guard.

The door slammed open again, this time loud enough to shake the lamps on the walls. As Cockram winced, all conversations in the room fell momentarily silent.

The man in the doorway stood a moment, looking abashed. He muttered something under his breath and turned to wrestle the door shut, fighting against the stiff ocean wind. Cockram rubbed his forehead as it thrummed with the aftershock of the bang, but the knot of tension in his chest eased. At last, the person he wanted to talk to had arrived.

The man had changed his clothing. Though the blood was washed from his hands, Todi's face was pale, his aspect twitchy. Having made fast the door, he hurried across the room, shoulders hunched, and slumped onto a stool in the darkest corner of the bar.

Conversation resumed as the wind changed its angle and rattled the shutters. Cockram pulled a tankard of ale and eased down the bar, setting the foaming brew in front of Todi.

The man didn't look up, only reached out with one raw looking hand and pulled the drink closer. His hair, short and ragged, was disheveled. His face had a stripped look to it, as if it had been scrubbed with a coarse cloth and harsh soap.

News of Billit's death had spread throughout Lan Dinas by now, offered up to key gossips by Cockram himself. Several other patrons cast covert glances at Todi as they murmured to their companions in lowered voices, and the man hunched lower on his stool, as if pressed low by the weight of their regard.

Cockram, lingering at Todi's end of the bar, selected a glass from the drying rack and began to polish it with his clean, white cloth. He didn't look at Todi, but he kept himself positioned so the man was in his peripheral vision. He'd made a study of men, and knew how to invite confidence without saying a word.

Todi raised his tankard and took a long, foamy draw, wiping his mouth with the back of his hand. He squeezed his eyes shut for a moment, scrubbing at them with a rough palm. At last, he let out a long, shuddering breath. "The rector's seen to everything," he said, speaking as if in answer to a question. "Billit's all taken care of, his family told what happened. Delari grant him peace."

Cockram raised the glass to the light, looking for smudges. Across the room, the four dock workers laughed. He lowered the glass and resumed polishing, keeping his tone neutral. "What about the tree, Todi? Is it felled? Or nearly so?"

Todi had raised his tankard for another swig of ale. He nearly choked at Cockram's words. Swallowing, he released a hoarse laugh. "Felled? Hardly that. Have you ever seen those monsters? That axe barely nicked the bark. Three strokes was all he managed. The fourth swing found Billit's poor leg instead."

Four strokes. Cockram considered this, surprised. He had known some ill would come of the scheme he'd encouraged Billit to hatch, but hadn't guessed the forest's retribution would be so swift, or so direct. He'd expected Billit to succeed in felling one of the great trees and for the fallout to come later, in a different form.

Still, this outcome wasn't without its advantages. A man's death could be the spark Cockram needed. If directed correctly, it could start the blaze he had been preparing for since the night he'd lost his eye.

He spoke again, choosing his words, pitching them in a tone that suggested he was thinking aloud more than having a conversation with Todi. "Funny, the timing. The forest hasn't taken a soul in generations. Now this happens, right after some among us have gained new powers."

Todi let out a sound that was half sob, half laugh. "Well, you can't say poor Billit didn't go looking for it. He broke every rule, did everything we all know not to do. It's no surprise, what happened. We're warned about those trees, aren't we? From the time we can walk, we know. We tell our own children about that place. Don't go near, don't go past the first trees. And even the woodcutters only gather what falls on its own."

Annoyed, Cockram set his glass on the shelf behind the bar and selected another from the drying rack. He shifted his argument. "But why should there be rules? Why should there be places on our own island where our children can't play? Billit was right. There's a fortune in timber sitting there, untouched. Why shouldn't we harvest Delari's bounty? That forest is a blight on Cynnes Tarth."

Todi, shaking his head, gulped more ale. "Say what you like, but I'm done. I'm not going anywhere near those trees again as long as I live. I'll stay up here by the ocean, where it's safe."

Cockram shook his head, setting his cloth and glass aside and placing his palms on the bar, leaning forward. "When I was a boy," he said, "I read a book about magic. Do you know what I learned? Like a thrown stone will always fall to ground and water will run always downhill, magics are governed by their own laws. And the most important one is magic cannot cast itself. There has to be direction for a spell to work. There has to be someone to point the power. There has to be a magician." He emphasized the last word, keeping his voice low but forceful.

Todi blinked, squinting as he tried to process the implication. He was quiet for a time, staring down into his mug. Finally he answered in a tentative tone. "But there's no one like that here, no one who could cast a spell and make an axe hit a leg instead of a tree."

Cockram waited a beat, letting Billit consider his own words. "There wasn't," he corrected. "There wasn't anyone here who knew about magics. Until the Tessilari girl arrived."

CHAPTER 3

The hidden city of Gol Ledrith was ancient, stately, and overflowing. Every morning, when Braven awoke, he looked up at the pattern of light dancing on the ceiling of his bedchamber. Here, at the heart of the forest, the fog was thin and airy. The sunlight spilled down over the narrow, jagged lake, illuminating the structures built upon its shores, the floating bridges, the soaring trees that grew up on every side in a protective ring, and rearing mountains beyond. Every morning, Braven lay in his bed for a moment and wondered what was to become of his city, his people.

The morning after the incident with the man in the woods, the question lay even more heavily on his mind than usual. Every aspect of what had transpired troubled him. First, there was the conversation he'd overheard. The idea that some in Lan Dinas were looking at the woods as a source of timber made him shudder with a blend of anger and fear. Then there was that sound – the terrible bite of axe in wood. It seemed to echo in his memory.

He could remember, also, the texture of the spell he'd woven, the heat and sting of it as he'd let it go into the world. He could remember the final thump, the gasp of pain, the confusion and horror. Braven had seen the blood spill, watched the axe fall from the man's limp fingers, heard the cries of pain. The once boastful man had collapsed in a writhing heap until his two companions could gather him up and haul him out of the woods.

They'd left the axe. It had lain there, gleaming in the dim air, until Braven had turned and walked away.

He had done the right thing. He knew that. The woods were the one defense his people had, the only barrier standing between Gol Ledrith and discovery. The people on this island could not be allowed to trespass on the trees. For centuries, the islanders had avoided the forest. If they did so out of fear rather than awe and respect, it had never mattered. The woodcutters came in a short way and collected downed limbs. Everyone else stayed away. That was how it had always been.

Until today. Braven couldn't remember ever hearing of men with axes coming to the forest with intent to cut down a living tree. He couldn't remember another Brinlock ever taking such an active role in turning such intentions aside.

He would have to report what had happened. He should have done it yesterday. He knew there would be no punishment for him. While Braven and his fellow Keepers were encouraged to scare those who ventured into the woods rather than kill them, people were injured and even died as a result of the misdirection spells woven into the woods. This was known and accepted as necessity.

Still, Braven's intervention had been far more direct than the usual techniques used by the Keepers. He had cast a spell and caused an axe to bite into a man's leg. How bad an injury had it been? Braven didn't know, but if the wounded man had died, it was because Braven had killed him.

Sitting up, Braven threw back his light sheet and stepped onto the smooth wooden planks of the floor. Gia, in her habitat, swam in a few excited circles before crawling up the stem of a reed to cry a greeting.

Smiling, Braven went to her. She stepped onto his hand, her skin warm and slick against his palm. She curled her sinuous body around his finger and let out a happy coo. He could feel her contentment seeping into him like a salve. "Come on then, love. I need that hand if I'm going to dress." He'd slept, as always, in his undershorts. His sleeping chamber was warm, kept so by the steam that rose off the water of Gia's pool. Each room in the house had such a place for her, the individual basins connected by a slim trough that snaked from room to room. It drew water from the lake, flowing always with a quiet current. It had an intake and output, and the water was pulled through the trough by a series of spells set into the grain of the light wood. This way, Gia could follow him throughout the house, all without growing uncomfortably dry.

Braven didn't have much of an understanding of the quiet, steady magic that allowed the wood to pull the water, to keep it moving, keep it warm, and give him and Gia a way to stay comfortably together any time Braven was at home. It took decades of study to learn the art of the woodsmiths, plus a great deal of precision and discipline. Braven's own magic didn't lend itself to the art. His strength was quick casting, improvisation, and agility.

He remembered again that feeling of heat, the prickle of the magic he'd thrown at the man in the woods just before the axe fell. He felt suddenly sick. Gently, he set Gia back on the reed, turning to pull on his trousers. The window was open, but he felt suddenly stifled. He pulled his shirt on and strode from the room, fumbling with the laces on his sleeves as he walked.

Braven's house was nothing spectacular, but as he pushed aside the sliding screens that led onto his wrapping porch, he felt a little rising sense of pleasure at the view. Gol Ledrith gleamed in the fog filtered morning sunlight, the pale heartwood of the structures luminous with reflected light from the lake.

The city was built atop and along a lake that lay deep within the ancient forest at the base of the craggy mountains that reared up on Cynnes Tarth's north end. It was a warmlake, with a population of brinlins and steam rising off the surface. It was connected to the other warmlake, the one near Lan Dinas, by a long, twisting river that ran tepid, but not warm.

Each building in Gol Ledrith stood on slender stilts. Each building was made of fine, white lumber harvested from sacred trees that had died of natural causes. Each building had a network of basins, just like Braven's house did, that pulled water from the lake and carried it throughout the interior, allowing brinlins to circulate among their people wherever they chose. Each home was connected to one of the major walkways by a delicate, arched bridge.

The city was built mainly along the shoreline. Some of the larger, more elaborate buildings extended over land and up the steep slopes of the banks, some reaching into the trees themselves and intertwining with trunks and branches.

Braven had never seen the other city—the one called Lan Dinas—that was built between the other warmlake and the shore of the cold, bitter ocean. He was told the houses were squat, earth-bound things made of stone, with rooms set on top of rooms and doors bound shut by iron. He had a hard time understanding why any person would choose to live in such a place. But then, he also had a hard time understanding how a man could take an axe and swing it at a living tree.

Braven strode out onto his porch and leaned against the railing, watching the slow heave of the lake's surface and trying to settle his thoughts. Gia popped up out of the water below him and swam in circles, attracting a clutch of wild brinlins that caught her pattern and flowed around her to become a liquid, many-colored shape.

Braven drew in a breath, trying to clear his mind. He stood like that for a long while, feeling the fog caress his face and letting the shush of the lake sooth him.

"Was it you?"

The voice broke him out of his meditation. It sounded from right beside to him, startling him badly. He turned, jerking towards the speaker. With an unpleasant shock, he saw he was no longer alone on his small balcony. Adni stood next to him, leaning on the rail just as he was doing, her gray cloak falling in a soft drape around her body.

Delari's breath, but the woman was spooky.

Braven felt his chest grow tight again, that pressure coming back into his heart. He hated being startled. He replied, not bothering to keep his annoyance out of his voice. "There's no need to sneak up on people."

Adni didn't look at him. She acted as if she'd barely heard him. She had dark hair and light eyes, and a firm, lean build. She went on. "He died, you know." Her voice was matter-of-fact and devoid of emotion, as if they were speaking about the weather. "I saw his corpse. I tracked his party back to the woods. I found a fallen axe, caked in blood. It was in your sector."

Adni watched the color drain from Braven's face, feeling a mild sense of satisfaction at his evident shock. Braven was one of the Keepers, and the Keepers, as a rule, did not approve of Adni. They did not appreciate the risks she took, the freedom with which she moved about the forest, Gol Ledrith, and Lan Dinas alike. Because they did not approve of her, mostly, they ignored her.

Braven was an untroubled soul. Like almost everyone else in this place, he'd been born here in the hidden city. He'd grown up playing in the warm shallows, encouraged to form a bond with a brinlin as soon as possible. He had never known the yearning, the confusion, or the fear that had marked Adni's own childhood.

On top of all that, Braven was young. He was known for his easy optimism and flexible casting. Taking all of this together, he was not exactly the ideal partner for Adni's needs. Still, she wasn't going to squander opportunity when it appeared.

Braven had gone stiff when she'd dropped her passive echo spell. He was said to be strong – a gifted caster. And yet, she'd snuck up on him without trouble. What she'd done was impolite, of course. No. It was worse than impolite. Using concealing magic was frowned upon in Gol Ledrith, if not overtly forbidden. But these little demonstrations of her own strength gave Adni confidence. They were also the primary reason she was so unpopular among her peers.

She waited a moment, making sure her words sank in. Braven was not slow on the uptake. His jaw tightened and he looked away from her, directing his gaze towards the distant shoreline. "He was trying to chop down a tree. I did what I had to do."

Adni adjusted her cloak, pushing it back behind her shoulders so her arms were free of the clinging fabric. She wore a sleeveless tunic, her bare skin exposed from the shoulder down. She stretched, somewhat theatrically. "Oh, I don't blame you. I'd have killed all three."

Braven didn't even favor her with a glance. She could see a vein pulsing in his neck. His voice was tight and unfriendly. "And that is why you're not a Keeper."

The comment stung. Adni drew in a slow breath, refusing to let him see his remark had hit home. It was what she'd wanted most in her younger years: to rove among the great trees and keep this haven safe from the murderous, treacherous townspeople. Gol Ledrith needed protecting more than the people here were willing to admit.

Which was why Adni hadn't been content to take up a trade or a husband, to settle down in this beautiful place and let her terrible memories of the past fade. The people who had betrayed her were still alive, unchanged, unchallenged, untried. As far as they knew, they'd gotten away with murder. She hadn't been their first victim, either. They would kill again. It was just a question of when and how and who.

For years after she was denied a place among the Keepers, Adni had coveted Vailria's post. Vailria lived at the edge of the forest in a little house on the shores of the warmlake. She knew the townsfolk, spoke to them, traded with them, and—most importantly—watched them. She watched for signs one among them was changing, as Adni had done all those years before.

It wasn't Vailria who had saved Adni's life, but her predecessor. Old Mino, he'd been called. He'd been well-liked among the islanders, and Adni remembered him from her earliest days. He had used to walk along the shore of the warmlake, leaning on a long staff he'd woven out of reeds. He would come upon her wading in the shallows and wink at her. She wouldn't worry. Although she wasn't supposed to be down by the water, she somehow knew he wouldn't tell.

She didn't remember much of the night he'd come for her, the night they would have killed her, the night Lan Dinas believed she died. She'd been delirious by then, racked with fever and weak with heat and confusion. She could remember lying in her damp bed. She could remember her brother's face. He would come into her room and stare at her sometimes, his expression flat and hopeless. She wanted to ask him to take her down to the warmlake, so she could see Bol one last time. But she'd been too dry, too spent. She'd looked up into his eyes and heard the toll of the death bell.

Then, there was magic. She could recall the prickle of it – the first time she'd felt a weaving take hold of her. From there, things grew blurry.

The next thing she remembered, she was sitting in the sand, bare feet in the warm shallows, Bol making his quiet, happy cheeps as he clung to her toe. She looked up, trying to remember. Had she made her request of her brother after all? Had he brought her here? Saved her?

There was a shape behind her, dim in the fading light. She'd turned, thrilling with happiness, ready to thank Cockram for doing what she'd been unable to ask.

But it hadn't been her brother whose gentle hand rested on her back, supporting her. It was Old Mino, his face creased with fatigue and sorrow. He'd helped her into a little boat he untethered from a hidden place among the thick reeds, and rowed her upriver to Gol Ledrith. There, it had taken the healers five days of working around the clock before they declared she would live.

It had been years before she knew the full story. It was Mino who told her, days before his own death. He'd come back to Gol Ledrith by then, Vailria having taken over his post. He was giving in to his age, his body failing. Adni visited him often, listening to his rambling tales, his weak voice underscored by the heave and lap of the lake.

He said it out of the blue one evening when they sat together drinking foamy tass from delicate earthenware cups and watching the trees seem to catch fire with the setting sun. He spoke without warning into a comfortable silence. "It was poison. Not illness."

Adni, drink cupped in her palm, shifted to look at him, then sat up a little straighter. Mino's eyes, often vague in those days, were sharp, focused, and haunted. His hair was gray and thin, the lines in his face deep and familiar. "They had given you poison, bit by bit, for days. That was why you nearly died."

The words, barbed and pregnant with implication, pierced a small hole in Adni's heart, crawled in, and took up residence. In the years to come, they would fester there, spreading blight and hatred and a thirst for revenge.

At that moment, she was too surprised to do more than echo his words. "Poison? What do you mean?"

Mino straightened, sitting up and stretching his thin back. He looked away from her, as if regretting his decision to speak. "The rector gave it to your brother, and your brother put it in your tea, as he was told to do."

Adni's heart began to pound. A sick feeling started in her stomach and spread a chill across her skin. She stood up suddenly. "My brother?"

Mino did look at her then. His eyes were full of shadows and sadness. "Cockram." His voice was steady, if weak. "He'd have seen you dead if I hadn't intervened."

Now, years later, Adni felt her eyes sting at the memory. Ever since she'd learned the truth, Adni had worked her way towards one, ultimate goal. Now, she thought that goal was within reach. But she needed an ally, a partner

Braven's act of violence, his angry mistake, was her chance. Perhaps the only one she'd ever have.

She chose her words carefully, not looking at the young man at her side. "Do you know what's happening in town because of what you did?"

✜

Marim stared at the jumble of her belongings spread out across the bed. She hadn't touched most of them in months. It had been two days since her conversation with Embriem on the shore of the warmlake, and she'd finally come to a decision.

Marim was packing. It was strange to pull all the items she'd stashed in the wardrobe back out into the light. With a sense of mystified disbelief, she touched a small, spangled purse with an open neck, watching as the slivers of reflective glass sewn into its seams glittered in the light of the lamps. She'd bought the thing not long before leaving Deramor. The design had recently come into fashion among Tessilari women. With open throated, sleeveless gowns worn at court, the little clutches gave a lady's tessila somewhere to ride.

The gown that went with the clutch was there also, hopelessly creased from its time in her sea bag. She knew there was a social scene here in Lan Dinas. Now and then, she saw Embriem go out dressed in a suit that would have been fashionable in Deramor a few seasons before. Those nights, she would sit in her room after she handed Tassin off to his nurse and wonder why he never invited her to go with him, never offered to introduce her into the society of the island.

She supposed it was because she was a governess. Her position as trained Tessilari and academy graduate was an automatic ticket into the court at Deramor, but here she had no such status.

Embriem had no reason to take her with him. She knew that. Still, it stung a little.

Now, gazing at all the things she'd hauled with her to this island, Marim couldn't help but remember the dreams she'd had, setting out. She'd thought she would be on the sea for months and months, visiting island after island, meeting strange people, seeing wild landscapes, using her healing magic to ease pain and maybe even save lives wherever she went. She'd thought she would come home with so many exotic tales, the other Tessilari would have to notice her, have to show an interest in her.

It all seemed so foolish now.

The agitated annoyance she'd been feeling since her conversation with Embriem by the warmlake surged through her again. In one quick swipe, Marim tossed the little clutch into the sea bag along with the other items she'd decided to leave behind.

Embriem had said he would not go to the forest, would not search for others like himself and his son. But he had no hold on Marim. As he'd stormed off from the lake, hauling Tassin after him, his question about her throat stinging as surely as if he'd struck her, Marim had realized something. She did not have to sit in this house and wait for a ship that might not come for another half year. She could do what she'd set out to do – broaden her horizons, make discoveries, explore.

On the desk, Marim's three tablets lay in a row, all bearing the same quick message she'd scrawled across each. "Have discovered the probable existence of a people like the Tessilari here. Think they have been hiding in the forest since the War of the Diods or maybe longer. Packing now, plan to try to find them."

So far, her words alone were written on each tablet, but as she tossed a pair of silk hose in with the clutch, she caught sight of letters forming on the third in line, the one without a seal in the corner.

Abandoning her packing, Marim hurried to the desk. Kix leapt into flight as she moved, leaving the spare bootlaces he'd been playing with to sweep across the room and catch hold of her shirt sleeve. He swung there, dewdrop eyes aglitter as he gazed up at her. She gave him a quick scratch under the chin and stooped to read the words as they formed. As always with Coll, the answer was a little bit over-excited, a little bit off topic.

"Have you been able to discover if brinlin young hatch in or out of the water? Keep in mind their power appears to come from the lake. If you stay inland, you might have an advantage."

Almost before the sentence was complete, words began to appear on the second tablet as well. Professor's Liam's hand was neat and familiar, the very sight of it somehow comforting. "Be careful, Marim. Do not expect a friendly reception. If they have been hiding all this time, it is because they do not feel safe. Cornered, fearful people are dangerous."

She felt a little twitch of annoyance as she finished reading the message. Even though she'd told Professor Liam all about how Kix had shifted at last, healing himself and thus repairing the long-damaged connection between them, her old teacher still didn't seem to think she could take care of herself.

A message began to form on the final tablet, then. This one was in the formal hand of a trained scribe. It could have been written by any one of the several dozen staff members who worked in the academy's tableturie, receiving and sending communications on behalf of the academy as a whole. The message was but a single word. "Noted."

Meanwhile, words were still forming on the tablet without the seal, the hand growing untidier with each sentence. Marim smiled to herself. Coll always tended towards scrawl when he was in a hurry to get his thoughts down. "I'm a graduate now, as of yesterday. Getting bored here. Thinking of coming to you, to see the brinlins for myself."

Marim had been on the verge of turning back towards her packing, but Coll's words stopped her cold. She felt a strange rush of emotion – a tangled skein of feeling so snarled and confused she couldn't even begin to separate out the different components.

She tried to imagine it. Coll. Here. If he'd still been a little boy, Marim would have been thrilled at the idea of having him with her again. She cherished the memory of their old closeness, the way he'd always turned to her when he needed help or reassurance or support. Sometimes, when he came to her in the night to cry out his pain, he would stay after his tears were spent. Lying in the quiet darkness, he would ask her question after question. His mind, even then, had been relentless in its thirst for knowledge. He'd wanted to know everything about everything.

But Coll wasn't a boy any longer. He was a young man. Eighteen and tall, his magic fantastically strong, he was still driven by that same thirst for knowledge. What had been charming in a boy was a little spooky in a man. She tried to imagine him among these stifled people, stalking about the town, asking questions, wading out into the warmlake to study the brinlins.

She snatched up her scribis and wrote back, her own hand a little hasty. "Not yet. Let me see what I find in the forest first."

She hovered a moment, staring at the blank tablet, waiting for an answer. One minute passed, then another. Down the hall, down the stairs, she heard the rise and fall of the dire's head knocker on the front door.

The sound jangled in her heart. For half a moment, Marim was all but convinced it must be Coll himself, having somehow devised a way to spirit his body across land and water in an instant.

She heard the front door open and close, followed by footsteps coming up the stairs and down her hall. She found herself staring with frozen disbelief at her door. There was a sharp rap. She swallowed hard and said, "Come in."

The butler stepped into the room, inclined his head, and handed her a letter. "This arrived for you, my lady. Delivered up from the docks." She saw his eyes flick over the heaped up belongings on her bed, then studiously settle on the fog-obscured view out the window.

Flushing with embarrassment, Marim thanked the man, accepted the letter, and waited until he had withdrawn and closed the door. Then she looked down at what she held.

The paper was plain, folded but not sealed, her name written on the front in smeared pencil.

Heart still pounding, Marim read the brief message scrawled inside. "I'm sending this ahead via a local lugger. My route has changed. If you still require passage back to Masidon, my ship will dock at sunset on the third of Tynes."

It was signed by Captain Tommin, the man who had abandoned her on Cynnes Tarth in the first place.

Marim felt her heart twitch in a strange spasm. The third of Tynes was today.

It was well past noon by the time Vailria rowed out of the narrow channel of the river into the foggy, open expanse of the warmlake near Lan Dinas. She sighed and shifted on the wooden seat of her slender canoe, angling to her right so she stayed aligned with the shore. After six months of hearings, six months of defending herself and her actions, six months of hiding her fury and impatience as the Wheel tried to decide whether she was a hero, a menace, or merely someone who had done her best given tough circumstances, she was free at last. Free to return to her quiet little house that stood alone near the edge of the forest.

The Wheel, somewhat unexpectedly, had decided in her favor. A few choice Brinlocks, those most skilled at staying hidden and moving unseen, had confirmed her story that a Tessilari now lived with Embriem and Tassin. The learned leaders of Gol Ledrith had concluded Vailria could not possibly have been expected to prevail over a trained graduate of the academy and her tessila when two newly minted brinlings resisted her attempts to lead them to safety. Vailria had been outnumbered. More than that, she'd been dealing with extenuating circumstances. She had done the right thing. While she had not succeeded in bringing Embriem and his son to Gol Ledrith, she had tried. Though she'd failed, she had done so in a way that had not, at least, revealed the existence of Gol Ledrith to the wider world.

Cleared of any wrongdoing, Vailria had been granted permission to return to her post, to leave Gol Ledrith at last. Reports the Wheel shared with her indicated Embriem was not doing well. His health had not recovered from his time suffering from the hunger, his business was failing, and the townspeople were not warming to his strange new status as an adult man who had gained the ability to wield magics.

The Wheel, though it had decided Vailria's case, was still in deliberations over Embriem and his son. Some Brinlocks believed the two needed either to be brought in or eliminated, that letting them exist as they were, bound with brinlins but without training or guidance of any kind, was a serious danger. Others regarded the situation as an opportunity to see how the population of Lan Dinas would react to the idea of sharing their lives with a magical people.

Vailria, for her part, did not have an opinion. In the midst of her terrible confrontation with Marim, when she'd felt the pulse and snarl of the girl's angry magic, she had come to a decision of her own. Since then, she had merely been biding her time. Now that she was free of Gol Ledrith at last, she could begin to carry it out.

The current, sluggish on the river, now lapsed to nothing. With one last roll of her shoulders, Vailria began to work the oars again. The craft was no passive hulk of dead matter. It was made of heartwood with magic spun into the grain. It was light and responsive, leaping ahead like a restive horse when she rowed, amplifying her effort as its delicate white prow sliced through the fog.

Before long, she slowed, squinting through the mist and looking for the narrow opening in the reeds. She almost missed it, had to turn suddenly so the boat bumped and jounced against the thick stand of stems. Disrupted brinlins cried and leapt for the water, some of them landing onto her vessel to sit up and mewl at her in irritation before hopping off into the lake.

Vailria ignored them. She worked the oars, making her way through the hidden channel, deep into the stand of reeds. One final stroke, and she came into the small clearing with its thin dock. She tied the boat, picked up her pack, and stepped onto the worn planks of the dock.

The reeds had grown in close during her absence, and she had to shoulder them aside. At last, however, she stepped out into the foggy air above the warmlake and walked along the planking onto the porch of her house.

She always half expected to find fault with her small, simple dwelling after she spent time in Gol Ledrith. Her home was not made of heartwood. It was not a combination of graceful lines and airy open spaces, moveable screens and upturned rooflines. It was more conventionally designed so the townspeople here didn't look at it any more askance than necessary. It was simple and plain, but also square and solid and tidy. The wood was rich with oil, the stilts sturdy and straight. The glass windows glittered in the sifted sun, and the fog shrouded the peak of the roof, softening the entire scene.

Vailria's heart lifted as she crossed the porch and opened the front door. Inside, she took a quick turn through the rooms. Nothing was disturbed here. She had feared trespassers, either angry townsfolk or perhaps Marim come looking for her here. But it appeared if anyone had come, they had not ventured beyond the porch.

With a sigh, Vailria set her bag down in the large front room. Then, with her heart in her throat, she went to a shelf on the wall. A carved wooden box sat alone there. She took it down and carried it with her to a low chair. She settled into the seat, the box in her lap, and closed her eyes. She could feel the pulse of magic beneath her fingers, and that alone caused relief to bloom through her. Never had she failed to replenish the workings of the spell within for so long. She had not anticipated she would be kept in Gol Ledrith for so long, and hadn't taken the box with her because she knew there would be an investigation. She hadn't wanted it found on her person.

Not that there was anything illegal or inherently distasteful about the box. It was merely personal, connected to a part of Vailria's life no one in Gol Ledrith knew about.

She sat a moment longer, preparing herself for what was to come. Tok, who had left her for a swim in the warmlake as they exited the forest, appeared in the corner where the floor stopped and a stand of reeds grew directly from the warmlake into the room. He clambered his way up one of the thick stalks and peeped at her. She opened her eyes, gave him the hint of a smile, and opened the lid.

Inside the box was a tiny ship, expertly carved out of heartwood and nestled down into the folds of piece of soft blue cloth. All the months she'd been stuck in Gol Ledrith without the box, Vailria had tried to comfort herself with the logic that Tommin's voyages around the islands always lasted at least a year. There was no way she could miss him again.

Nevertheless, she'd worried. Now, as she opened the box, she saw what she had both hoped and feared.

The ship was glowing.

With a quick snap, Vailria closed the lid again. She sat staring ahead, shocked, feeling the familiar pulse of magic in her hands. She remembered the night she'd woven this spell, remembered pressing the other ship she'd carved out of the small, dear piece of heartwood into a square, blunt-fingered hand. She remembered whispering, "When you are three days out, hold this in your hand, like this, and say three times, 'I am coming.' Then I will always know to expect you."

Last time the ship had glowed, something had gone wrong. Tommin had put in at Lan Dinas, but then left before Vailria ever made it to the docks. She was determined this would not happen again.

The Wheel was divided, uncertain what the existence of Embriem and his son would mean for the island. But Vailria knew the people of this town better than the elders back in Gol Ledrith did. She knew how small-minded, how superstitious, how hateful they were. She had seen, first-hand, the quiet machinery that ran beneath the surface in this place. It spun to life slowly when someone dared to deviate, and didn't stop until it delivered death.

Vailria knew exactly what was going to happen in the coming months. She could feel it already, a mounting tension in the magic the warmlake breathed into the air. Something was building in this place: building and building and preparing to boil over.

Vailria replaced the box on its shelf. She would have no further need for the spell, yet she stopped short of deadening it, of pulling the magic out of the wood and turning it into a plain, lifeless trinket.

She looked around the room, trying to decide what to take with her. She caught sight of Tok on his perch. He was watching her, head cocked, his posture indicative of mild worry.

Her heart clenched, and she looked away. It was going to hurt them both, what she planned to do. It might even kill them.

But Vailria had had enough of waiting, of hiding, of skulking in shadows. It was time, at long last, to make a choice.

Embriem sat on the edge of his bed, holding a worn leather pack in his hands. It was small—smaller than he'd remembered—sized for a child. It had a simple flap closure and a leather tie. How many times had he opened it up, looked in at his lunch, and closed it again because the sun had not yet reached its peak in the sky? How many times had he set it beside himself on his cloak, his mother's book positioned carefully so he could snatch it out and open it if he heard someone coming, so he would appear to be studiously reading if Chalsia approached?

A light tapping intruded on his thoughts. He looked up to see Marim standing in the doorway, looking uncertain and a little untidy, her short hair half pulled back in a thong with shorter strands escaping all around her face. Still, she didn't wait for him to invite her in. "I need to talk to you." Her voice was serious.

Embriem set the bag aside, suddenly aware of how barren and plain his bedchamber must seem. He wasn't sure how long he'd been sitting here, or why he had this bag in his hands. He wasn't even entirely sure what day it was. This had been happening to him lately. He was losing time.

He rose, took a few steps towards Marim, and stopped to stare at the tall mirror that had once been Chalsia's. He knew Marim had come to tell him again all the things she'd already told him, to try to convince him to change his life.

But how could he change? Changing would mean moving on, leaving the man he'd been behind.

So Embriem spoke preemptively. "It's not that I don't want to go, Marim. It's that I *can't* go." He felt the need to explain, to defend himself against her unspoken accusation. "I belong here. I'm needed here. Look at this life I have built." He made a sweeping gesture, indicating his entire house. "I have staff in my home, I have staff in my warehouses. I can't just walk away. I can't go wandering off into the forest simply because you think there might be other people like me out there. You're not going either, Marim. Tassin needs you here."

That last was a mistake. Marim stiffened, her face hardening. Her tessila appeared, crawling out of her collar to dart up into the air and flit about the room, then land on her shoulder and hiss at Embriem.

"Kix." Marim spoke the creature's name in a mollifying tone. "Enough of that." But her own eyes were sharp.

The girl stood a moment, measuring him. "If you're so worried about Tassin, you should be searching for others like yourself. These bonds can be dangerous, you know." She gestured at Kix. "Overextension can be fatal. If Tassin experiments on his own, which I promise you he will, he will make mistakes. I don't understand his magic. It's not like mine. With only me to help him find his limits, there will be danger."

Embriem felt his jaw tighten. He stared at the mirror and thought, for a moment, he could see Chalsia standing there, looking back at him with her lifted chin, her eyes that always saw the best in him.

There was a pause. Watching him, Marim spoke again, her tone soft. "Is it your wife?"

Startled, Embriem felt a surge of strange hope, glancing at Marim with disbelief. For a moment, he thought Marim was looking at the mirror as well, that she could see Chalsia too.

But Marim was looking at him, not the mirror. She was looking at him with a strange mix of pity and disapproval. "You're not the only person who has lost someone, you know."

He looked away from her, suddenly angry. Marim had lost people, he didn't doubt. But she hadn't lost Chalsia.

She seemed to read his thoughts. Something in her eyes sparked. "You asked about my scars."

Embriem said nothing. He turned to stare at the wall, feeling the urge to leave but unable to walk past her to reach the door.

Marim continued. "They're from a collar I was forced to wear when I was kidnapped as a child. I wasn't yet ten, but it was the second time in my life I was taken away from everything I knew. The first time, I was Tassin's age, dying of the hunger. My parents had it too. We could have all been saved. It would have been the simplest thing. All we needed were tessili. But instead, my parents were murdered in their sleep by a girl who had, in her turn, been snatched from her home. I was taken to the academy and encouraged to bond with a tessila. If things hadn't changed, if the Tessilari hadn't risen again, if the academy as it was hadn't fallen, I would be a trained assassin now. I would be creeping into houses at night, killing parents and stealing children."

Marim's voice had grown tighter and tighter as the words spilled out of her, the underlying anger mounting. Her tessila leapt into the air to fly restless circles about the room. Embriem felt a brief, fierce wish for Nel. He pushed it aside.

Marim was breathing hard and her voice was shaking, but she went on. "Do you hear what I'm saying, Embriem? I'm telling you what I've seen. I'm telling you what happens to those who are feared. I'm telling you what societies will do to keep magics tamped down, keep them under control, keep them hidden. Do you think it's a coincidence you and your son are the first people known to bond with brinlins? Do you think the death serum the church doles out really has anything to do with mercy? How many children have been killed here? Children who could have simply been taken to the warmlake and allowed to discover their birthright."

Embriem felt a weary unease. He remembered the rector's words, his persuasive argument to allow the sisters to come to Tassin, to guide him peacefully into Delari's embrace. He remembered his own willingness to let it happen.

Marim's voice was an angry hiss. "A people does not go from systematically murdering and suppressing a deviant strain to simply accepting them into society. It took a war with a supernatural monster and a royal decree to get Masidon to accept the Tessilari, and still there is strife. There are families who try to murder their own children rather than see them bond with tessili."

Her words were targeted missiles, expertly aimed to blast their way through the layers of denial he'd been building and strengthening in the months since the first signs of Tassin's illness. Hurt, angry, confused, Embriem wheeled on Marim. "I'm not like you," he all but shouted. "I'm not strong. I'm not a survivor. I'm a merchant, a trader. All I know and love is here, in this house, in this town where I've always lived. What do you want from me?"

But even as he said this, Embriem recalled the memory that had only recently been returned to him – the memory of the time he'd gone into the dangerous woods and saved Tem Cutter, the strongest, cleverest, most successful man ever to work the forest. He'd done it for Chalsia. Or rather, he'd done it *with* Chalsia. She'd been the one determined to go into the woods in search of her father. He had merely gone along.

Marim, looking up at him, didn't so much as hesitate. She answered quickly, her tone sharp. "I want you to live. I want you to do what's best for your son and yourself. I want you to move past your grief." She paused, and her voice became gentler for a moment. "Moving on won't mean giving up loving her, you know."

It was all too much. Embriem felt suddenly too tired. His agitation faded to dullness. He was overcome by a numb feeling of defeat. If anyone knew how dangerous the woods were, it was him. How could he take Tassin there? Or even Marim? How could he hope to find a people who had successfully kept themselves hidden for centuries?

He sat back down on his bed. His body felt heavy. He stared at the floor, not seeing the rich hues of the tile. "No." He spoke with certainty. "I'm not going into that forest, Marim. Neither is Tassin. Neither are you. Not if you want to remain in my employ. I'm sorry."

CHAPTER 4

It wasn't often Cockram visited the outer neighborhoods of Lan Dinas. Although the people who lived in the simple houses built along the rutted streets were stout, solid, hardworking folk, they were not the kind of people Cockram preferred to spend his time with. They had little time to spare, and even less money. They had no space in their lives for the things Cockram appreciated, things like fine clothing and exotic food. As Cockram made his quick way among the rush-thatched homes, he had trouble believing he'd spent his boyhood on a street not so different from this one.

These people, he reminded himself, were not contemptible. They were a necessary part of the island's economy. They might be uncouth, unrefined, uneducated, but that was exactly what made them so useful.

He reached the end of the street and paused for a moment outside a yard. It was a tidy enough patch, with the house set back from the road and chickens scratching in the short grass. Cockram took note of the brand new sawhorse standing in brilliant glory off to one side of the front door, made of solid wood, sturdy and strong. The people who lived here could never have afforded such a thing, not with the price of timber. Cockram had sent it to them, a gift, along with the axe.

Now, he pushed through the woven reed gate and strode up the dirt path that led to the door. The walls were washed white, but they'd been made of rough, mud bricks mixed with chopped reeds. The door was of pressed reedwood, as were the window frames. The reeds were the one resource this place had in plenty, and the common people used them for every imaginable purpose.

Low light spilled out of the two front windows, lighting up the fog. Cockram touched his eye patch, assuring himself it was in place, and tapped on the door.

His knock was answered by a child, who cracked it only wide enough to show a grubby face with large, red-rimmed eyes and tangled hair. A voice said something from within. The child disappeared, leaving the door ajar. Cockram, unwilling to dither on the threshold, pushed his way inside.

The front room of the house was large and comfortable, even if the floor was packed dirt. It felt crowded, nevertheless, with its current population of two women, two children, and four men. Cockram had asked them to gather here. He felt strangely electrified as they all turned to look at him, their eyes full of sorrow and anger. The perfect emotions for him to direct.

Resisting the urge to smile, Cockram turned to close the door behind him. Then he stood up straight and did a quick scan of the faces.

Although he had never met some of the people here, it didn't take him long to place them all. There was Todi, of course, and Mart – the two unfortunate accomplices, both of whom Cockram had spoken to before now. Then there were the rest, all members of Billit's family, the man who had died trying to chop down a tree.

Billit's wife was middle-aged, as he had been, with streaks of gray in her bright red hair. She sat with one of her two grandchildren on her lap, but the look on her face was distant and abstracted, as if what was happening in the room was making only the vaguest impression upon her senses.

The third child, the one who'd opened the door, clung to the skirts of the other woman. That woman was younger, and she had the sour face of a person who is never satisfied.

Finally, there were the two young men. Billit's sons. They stood together, arms crossed, staring at Cockram with their father's bluster. It was the younger of the two who was married, Cockram knew. The older was unmarried, unemployed, and had been something of a thorn in his father's side.

Cockram knew all this because he'd done his research. He'd selected this family precisely for its many ideal qualities. The men were hot-tempered, the women were discontented, and the lot of them were keen to blame their troubles on anyone but themselves.

Billit had been easy to influence. All he'd needed was a few conversations to get him fired up, a sawhorse and an axe, and he'd gone off to attack a tree, convinced he'd make his fortune just that easily.

Now, Cockram felt the anger in the room, saw the boiling rage in the eyes of the whole family. Only Todi and Mart looked anything less than furious. They sat together in a corner, their bodies tense, their eyes sliding about the room as if looking for an escape route.

Cockram had been preparing and refining his opening line all the way down from the docks, and although one of the sons opened his mouth to speak as soon as Cockram stepped through the door, he pre-empted the man, raising his voice to drown out the first syllables of what could only have been an accusation. "Now, more than ever, we all here in this room have something in common."

He delivered his words with confidence, his voice ringing. They had the desired effect. The son who had been about to speak closed his mouth. Everyone present went still, waiting for him to go on.

"A tree cannot kill." Cockram moved a few more steps into the room and stopped in the center of the floor. "But magics can. Do you know what else magics can do?"

He paused for a moment, letting his question hang in the air. Then, he gestured at his eye patch. "They can take a man's eye, pluck it right out of his head." Watching the faces around him,

Cockram was pleased to see this revelation hit home. Expressions ranged from shock to horror to disgust.

He squared his shoulders and glared at his audience with his good eye. He'd been building up to this moment for six months. He'd diligently spread rumors and stoked fears. The Tessilari girl was already unpopular. Now, he was going to make her reviled.

"Yes," he said. "It's true. The witch attacked me that night, springing on me out of the storm. I have kept it a secret until now because I was ashamed. I was ashamed of my weakness, ashamed of my ruined face. But now that this has happened, now that she has hurt you too, I see I owe you the entire truth. If something is to be done about the abomination that has come here to spread foul corruption among our own, we must all acknowledge the hurt she's caused, the suffering she's doled out among us."

One of Billit's sons rumbled a wordless agreement, and the women were leaning forward, sour faces rapt. Only Mart and Todi weren't entirely won over. Their expressions were shuttered, not with disagreement, but with fear.

They didn't matter. Cockram had to work to keep a smile off his face. He had momentum now. He could feel it in the room, and he knew there were others all around town who were primed to hear the message that would start to spread the moment he left here tonight.

It was well and truly begun now. Cockram would have his revenge at last.

Braven hopped out of the canoe, wading through the shallow water towards the shore. Adni caught up her cloak in one arm and stepped into the water as well, standing by the reeds as she watched him make the boat fast by tying it off to a short stake jutting a few inches above the water. Then she showed him the all but invisible path through the reeds, the way the tall stems could be parted and shouldered aside until they gave way to the high grasses that grew on the shore. Both Brinlocks wore high, flexible boots infused with a weave that kept their feet dry, but Braven could feel the warmth of the water through the leather.

He stepped up onto the shore and turned. Gia had climbed up one of the reeds and was cheeping at him, her blunt head cocked as she watched him with keen curiosity.

Braven glanced at Adni. She had let her cloak out. She stood in the warm, heavy air with her bare arms crossed, gazing up the slope towards the row of houses that stood at the top of the rise. They were squat, unrefined buildings, but their windows threw soft light out into the fog.

There were other brinlins in the reeds, letting out their high, haunting cries. There were so many here. The reeds were thick with them, and Braven could feel the warmlake was so full of magic it practically hummed with a life of its own. A thought slipped into his mind, unbidden. *This is such a waste. We should be living on this shore as well, not all crowded into Gol Ledrith.*

Surprised at himself, Braven pushed the thought aside. He glanced at the other brinlins, but couldn't tell whether or not one of them was Adni's. He stood there, indecisive for a moment, then reached for Gia. With a pleased trill, she climbed onto his finger and into his sleeve to stow herself inside his cuff. "Stay out of sight, now." He whispered the words affectionately, then turned to Adni.

She hadn't moved. He didn't know if she had her brinlin with her, if the animal was hidden within the hood of her cloak, perhaps, or if it was happy enough to stay in the warmlake. Some brinlins were more independent than others.

There was the sound of a door slamming. Braven looked up to see a group of people moving along the horizon. They were only dim shapes in the fog, lit by the torches they carried. He felt a shiver of fear. He'd never been so close to Lan Dinas before. The woods were his domain. He did not leave the safety of the trees. He pulled his own cloak in a little, though it was not cold. He could hardly believe he was here, on this shore, so close to the city he'd avoided all his life.

Adni had come to him as the sun was setting to tell him it was time. She'd convinced him, during their previous conversation, the death he'd caused was going to spark a riot. Hatred and fear had been building among the people here since the night Vailria fled her post and returned to Gol Ledrith. Adni had been sent to Lan Dinas regularly since then, to gather intelligence for the Wheel. She knew and understood what no one else seemed willing to recognize. "Tensions have been building for months," she told him, "and this death is going to be like a spark on tinder. The Wheel is too slow, too complacent. They hear my warnings, but they do not act. I know how we can stop what's happening. We can steal the momentum, direct it against the real enemy."

He'd had questions, of course. Who, for instance, was the real enemy? But Adni put him off, saying she'd explain everything at the proper time.

It was guilt, more than anything, that made him go with her when she appeared at his door at sunset. He'd gone because he couldn't think of a way to say no, couldn't find it in himself to refuse to help her deal with a problem he himself had created.

Now, the voices he heard drifting through the fog were angry. He remembered the smack of that axe biting into the stately, ancient tree, remembered the heat of his spell as it left him, remembered the shriek of pain as metal bit flesh. He pushed the memories aside.

Adni spoke, low. "It's already begun."

She turned to Braven. There was a light in her eyes he'd never seen there before. Her cloak was a shifting blur against the fog, playing with his ability to focus his eyes. Her voice was low and firm, her gaze steady. "Your job tonight, your single, all-important goal, is to save a child's life. Do you think you can do that?"

Braven's first feeling at her words was one of profound relief. He wouldn't have to fight, wouldn't have to cast spells that could lead to the deaths of more people. *Save a child.* He almost laughed at the simplicity of it. But he caught the harsh glitter in Adni's face and schooled his emotions, bringing them back into hand. He spoke in a somber tone. "Yes. Of course. Of course, I can do that."

She nodded and extended her hand, passing a slip of heartwood paper into his palm. When he unfolded it, he saw a simple map. It was only a few lines, marking the warmlake and the streets he should follow. His current location was indicated by a glowing dot that pulsed on the lake's edge. "His name is Tassin. He and his father, Embriem, are brinlings. The father might refuse to come." Adni paused, staring into the dark as if choosing her words carefully. "One way or another, we can't abandon the boy. Bring him back here, with or without his father. Take him to Gol Ledrith. Don't wait for me. If you don't get him out of here, he's unlikely to survive the night."

Braven nodded, feeling decidedly less settled about his task already. This "saving" sounded an awful lot like kidnapping.

Still, he did not argue. He folded the paper in on itself. He looked at Adni, seeing the set of her jaw, the tension in her shoulders. "What are you going to do?"

Her answer came back so low he almost couldn't make out the words. But he did hear, and her answer made the vestiges of his relief vanish like smoke hit by a stiff wind.

"First, I'm going to kill the rector. After that, it's time for my brother to face the tiger he's been baiting all these months."

Sometimes, Marim felt any grit she might have had as a person had been used up during the terrible days she'd spent with Nylan, wearing a collar and watching Kix inch ever closer to death. She had survived that ordeal, somehow, but since then she seemed to lack tenacity. If was Professor Liam's most consistent criticism of her spellwork. She could well remember the way he would look at her when she lost her grip on a weaving. He would say in his gentle voice, "Marim. You let go too easily."

He hadn't known, hadn't been able to understand the way the connection between her and Kix had been damaged when they'd both nearly died. He'd had no concept of the struggle it had been for her to draw enough magic into herself to use even in the smallest of castings. He'd thought her lack of success had to do with a lack of grit, a lack of strength.

Maybe he'd been right. Because Marim was giving up now.

After her fruitless conversation with Embriem, she'd returned to her own room. Lying there on her desk, Tommin's note had seemed like a sign. She'd gone to Tassin and sat with him for a few hours, trying her best to tell him everything he might need to know about magic in the days to come. She'd taken her leave of him, eyes hot and stinging, without ever telling him the truth.

She'd gone to the kitchens and begged a cold dinner of ham and bread and cheese. The cook gave her one, face flinty with displeasure. Marim returned to her room, where she shoved everything she owned back into her sea bag.

The sun was falling now, lighting the fog with its lurid glow. Marim had her window open. Kix was flying in and out, dancing on the heavy air. He would not be happy when he realized they were to board the ship again, to once more spend months on the blank ocean, crammed in among men who looked at them askance and made gestures of warding when they thought she wasn't looking.

But after that, after the long journey, Marim would be back in Masidon. The ride from the coast to Deramor wouldn't be so bad. Kix would have the fields and forests to flit around in. They would have fresh air and solitude. Eventually, they would enter familiar territory. Marim imagined riding up to the cheesery, seeing her grandmother's face light up when she realized who had come. Her grandfather would come banging in from the back, smelling of whey and fresh grass. They would hug her and kiss her cheeks and she would stay with them for a day or two. Then, she would go to the academy. Coll would be there, waiting to hear about everything she'd seen.

She had to go. She had to go because it was no longer safe here. Embriem was too stubborn, too locked in his own grief to see the signs, to notice what was building in the atmosphere. Several times today, she'd looked out her window to see small knots of people standing on the lane at the top of Embriem's drive, muttering among themselves and casting dark looks at the house.

If Embriem would not try to save himself, Marim had to save her own skin and get out of here.

Her only regret was Tassin. She felt an urge to take him, to spirit him away and deliver him to the academy where wiser minds than hers could teach him to use his strange power. But even if she could have brought herself to separate him from his father, to take him from this place would be nothing short of murder. He needed his brinlin, and his brinlin needed the warmlake.

So, Marim would go alone. She would walk away with nothing to show for her time here except more memories to weigh her down, to eat at her in the quiet hours before dawn when, if she was unlucky enough to wake, the past seemed to loom large in her psyche, strong and brittle and full of her failures.

She was done packing. She sat on the edge of the bed in the room that had begun to feel a little like home. Outside, the light was fading, swallowed up moment by moment by the fog. She was beginning to wonder what she would do if the ship was late, if she had to live another day or two in this house, when she heard the harbor bell. It was distant but clear in the still air, pealing out the notes that meant a trade ship had arrived.

Marim was on her feet, her sea bag slung over her shoulder, feet heading for the door, before the last echo of its notes had faded to silence.

Adni knew the rector's habits. He was a predictable man, with his movements connected to the rhythm of the life of the cloister and the needs of the three gods his church served. His patterns of behavior had not been difficult to learn. Adni had been shadowing him, haunting his steps, since she'd first slipped out from under the eye of the Wheel and come back to Lan Dinas mere days after Old Mino's death.

The rector, in Adni's view, was the worst kind of man. He was a man who preached Delari's message of love, Priam's code of honor, and Tristis' promise of eternity. His cloister educated the children of the poor, provided medicine to the ill, and positioned itself as a benevolent presence on the island.

But Adni knew better. Dinon was no kind-hearted patriarch. He was a killer – a man who had practiced deliberate genocide for decades. How many brinlings had he disposed over the years? How many times had the Watcher here in Lan Dinas been too late to stop the kiss of death from falling on the lips of a child who could have lived?

For years, Adni had held her hand for one reason. Dinon was one of many. He was acting not of his own accord, but in response to long established instructions laid out in the Vaulted Father's Directive. If she killed Dinon, another rector from Elys Yins would only step in and continue the same work. If Adni killed him as well, there would be another, and another after that. She did not know the origin of the order to kill, didn't know where the hatred came from. But she did know it hadn't started with Dinon. It wouldn't end with him, either.

Adni had waited for decades. She'd stood in the shadows, biding her time. She'd known, all along, there would be a time—the right moment—to take her revenge when Dinon's death would do the most good.

It was here at last.

She and Braven parted ways when they reached the path. They said nothing, only caught eyes for a second before setting off in different directions. His task would lead him into town, across the high street and up to the large house where a man and a boy who belonged in Gol Ledrith did not realize they were in danger.

Adni moved on her soft boots towards the rectory. She carried no light, and the fog was thick and soft against her face. She knew the way well, and moved with certainty. She'd left Bol behind. He would be safer in the warmlake. Still, she felt a little stab of longing for his presence as she moved at a light jog uphill from the shore.

It wasn't long before the tall, graceful outline of the cloister buildings reared up out of the fog in front of her, sudden and massive, black shapes in an already dim sky. Adni knew where Dinon would be. She'd heard him and Cockram discuss their plans. As she moved up to the stone wall and skirted towards the rector's personal quarters, she reached beneath her cloak and drew out a long, slim tube. Then she proceeded across the tidy grounds and sidled, at last, up to a window.

The glass was open, as usual. The scent of incense drifted out, pungent and sharp. Adni eased her way up to the panes and peeked inside.

Dinon stood in front of the large mirror that occupied the main wall of his living quarters, practicing his speech. He always practiced his sermons this way, trying out modulations and cadences, deciding the precise way to roll the words off his tongue. Usually he spoke of harmony and forgiveness, of peace and honor and generosity.

Tonight's message would be different, but Adni did not stop to listen. She was already behind. Up the slope, in town, the fog was lit with a lurid brightness. Groups of people were moving in the streets, carrying torches, heading for the square where Dinon would, as he'd said, "Incite them to riot."

She caught a few words as she carefully plucked her supply of poisoned darts from the pouch on her belt, rolling open the thin layer of enchanted suede that kept her safe from the magical toxin. She selected a dart, set the rest on the windowsill, and dropped the sharp, pointed, projectile into the copper tube. She waited a moment as Dinon's voice rose and fell. She picked up on a word or phrase here and there. "Abomination ... corruption ... godless ways."

Adni settled herself by the open window and raised the dart gun to her lips. She'd practiced with this weapon for hundreds of hours, always imagining this moment – her chance to destroy the man who had turned her own brother's hand against her.

She drew in a breath, stilled her body, and blew.

The dart flew true. Nevertheless, Adni was already reloading as the Rector's flow of words broke off and he slapped at his neck where the dart had struck. "What in …?" His tone was irritated. Confused. He turned to the open window.

Adni fired again. The second dart hit him square in the soft flesh of his wrinkled throat. The third sank into the back of his hand.

Dinon brushed the darts away. They fell, landing with soft thumps on the plush rug. He began to walk towards the window, brows drawn together. "Who's there?"

Adni did not hurry. She rewrapped her remaining darts in their slip of suede and stowed them back in the pouch. She slid the blow gun into its sleeve within her cloak.

"Reveal yourself, or I will call the city guard." Dinon had stopped a few feet from the window. His voice was querulous, thinner now he wasn't performing.

She leaned forward so he could see her fully. "Only one of your murdered children, come back to say hello." She hoped he could see the hate in her eyes, hoped he could feel how much she'd wanted to kill him all these years.

Dinon was squinting. The poison in the darts affected the nervous system. All his senses would be failing within another few seconds. She hoped he had a chance to get a good look at her face before his vision dissolved into white snow.

The rector said nothing, did nothing. The old man she'd hated for so long stood a moment longer, then collapsed onto the floor with a soft moan.

Not wasting any time, Adni heaved herself up and through the window. She dropped into the room and stepped over the prostrate rector to retrieve her darts. She pulled a different pouch out of her belt, a leather glove, and a small pair of copper tongs. Gingerly, one at a time, she picked the poisonous barbs out of the carpet and dropped them into the bag. Then she stowed all her equipment and scanned the room for any lingering sign she'd been there.

She checked for a pulse in the rector's neck on her way back to the window. The man was dead.

Adni felt her lips twitch into a smile. She looked out the window, towards the town. "Now brother," she said. "It's your turn."

CHAPTER 5

Embriem was in his study, slumped at his desk like a discarded rag doll. Marim approached the door with reluctance, feeling a cowardly desire to simply slip out the front door and away. But this man had taken her in when everyone else would have turned her away. He'd housed her and fed her, even paid her.

Outside, the sun was falling fast. The fog was thick and lurid with the late light. It seemed the sky above the neighboring rooftops was lit from below as well. This made Marim inexplicably uneasy. *I must get to the ship,* she thought. *It's time Kix and I were away from this place.*

Drawing up outside the open office door, Marim tapped on the frame. Embriem did not respond. He sat as if the animating force had gone out of him entirely. For a moment, Marim wondered if he was dead, if something had happened to his brinlin and the two joined souls had been called back to Tristis' domain.

Just when she was convinced something was truly wrong, Embriem turned. He swiveled around in his fine wooden chair, but he did not look up. He looked terrible – his face grooved with lines of fatigue, his eyes over-bright and unfocused. *This isn't the right way for them to live, always away from their brinlins,* Marim thought. *He can't go on like this much longer.*

Embriem stared at the floor, saying nothing. Marim found herself wavering. *This man needs help.*

But then she remembered their conversation earlier. Trying to persuade him was hopeless. She'd made her decision, and she would follow through. "I'm sorry," she said. "I must leave you now. My ship has returned. I've decided to go back to Masidon. Thank you for everything."

He didn't react at first. For a moment, she thought he would not. She turned, prepared to walk to the front door, step out into the evening, and walk away from this place with never a word of acknowledgment from the man whose roof she'd lived under for half a year.

She'd all but taken her first step when Embriem looked up, blinking. His eyebrows pulled together. His eyes, red-rimmed and brilliant, focused on her at last. "What do you mean, you're leaving? Who will teach Tassin?"

It stung her, somehow, that the only argument he could muster had to do with his son. He didn't say, "What about that day you came to me in the fog and showed me how to save myself? What about when we faced down Vailria together and sent her packing?"

No. It was as if those things had never happened. It was as if she really was a governess, brought here for the sole purpose of teaching young Tassin how to read and write and do sums.

In the doorway, Marim stood up straighter. She looked at Embriem's grooved face, at his pale skin and gaunt frame. She understood something she hadn't realized until now. She spoke the knowledge the moment it came into her mind. "You will die, Embriem. You first, Tassin a little later. You can't live like this, always apart from your brinlins, going to the warmlake for only a little time, once or twice a day. It's killing you by inches. Tassin's magic isn't like mine. Neither is yours. You need help. You need guidance from someone like you. If we go now, if we leave tonight to find the people who live in the forest, I will go with you. Otherwise, I'm heading for the docks. I can't live in this house and watch you and your son run out of time."

Embriem's eyes grew sharper as she spoke. She thought she was getting through to him at last. She imagined, suddenly giddy, what it would be like in the forest. They would go together: a team. It might take weeks to search out this ancient, hidden people. They would live by their wits, driven by necessity. They would come out of it changed, knowing each other like no one else did.

But she'd misunderstood the look in his eyes. As she finished talking, that light faded. He turned away from her and directed his empty gaze back out the window. "I already told you. I'm not leaving." His voice was hollow. "I will die here, if it comes to that."

There was no use arguing. So, Marim left. "Good-bye, Embriem." She spoke the words quickly and didn't wait for an answer. She walked away from the open office door and into the entry hall that had once struck her as so grand. Now it seemed cold. Dim. Empty.

The front door swung heavily when she pushed. She turned to close it behind her and saw the knocker she'd noticed the first day – the disembodied head of a ferocious animal, holding a ring its mouth.

Marim closed the door. The fog seemed to shoulder in all around, filling her lungs with damp and warmth, the scent of leaves and rust. She pulled up her hood, shouldered her ungainly bag, and began to walk.

Something was wrong. Cockram had done his part. His months of dropped hints and crafty insinuations had prepared the way, creating a sense of resentment and unease among the people of Lan Dinas. Now, Billit's death had scared them. Cockram had worked to stoke that fear, to direct it and give it a target.

Hatred was smoldering in the crowd that had gathered in the square. The people who had answered Cockram's call were not the fine folk who typically did their shopping here in the grander parts of the city. These were the men and women who lived at the fog-filled edges of things, who worked the lakeshores or the rim of the forest or, in the case of the woodcutters, the forest itself.

They were here. They were ready. Cockram stood at the back of the raised platform at the edge of the town square where city officials delivered the municipal announcements every week. The city guard was there too, drawn up around the edges of the restless crowd. Some, Cockram could see, were sympathetic, their eyes as eager as the people who had come here. Others looked nervous. They stood fingering their clubs and keeping an eye on escape routes. There wasn't much need for law enforcement in Lan Dinas, and these men had no experience dealing with mobs.

The scene was set, the fire laid. All they needed now was one final push.

The rector was supposed to be here. His words would push these people over the edge, give their anger permission to overflow into violence and seal the Tessilari girl's fate.

But the rector had not come. He'd promised to address the crowd at sunset, but the lurid light in the sky was beginning to fade, the people beginning to shift and murmur in restless confusion. If someone didn't speak to them soon, they would disperse. The moment would fade with the light in the sky. All his work would come to nothing, after all.

Cockram, watching two women in gray dresses whisper to each other behind their hands, felt a prickle of premonition. All this time, he'd assumed the Tessilari girl was ignorant. He'd been making his plans believing she'd been paying him no attention. He'd believed her complacent. He'd thought she'd be an easy mark.

Now, unease crept over him. He reached out and hauled a boy out of the crowd, pressed a coin into his hand, and hissed an order in his ear. The boy looked up at his face, down at the coin, then back up at Cockram. "As fast as you can," Cockram said. "Go."

The boy took to his heels, shouldering his way through the crowd until he could reach a side street and open into a run. Cockram watched him race away, then looked back at the crowd. Even if the boy did return with the rector, it would be too late. The people had gathered to hear someone speak. They would not linger if the heat went out of the moment.

With a sharp intake of breath, Cockram made his decision. Unfolding his arms, he stepped forward on the platform, blinking as torches threw their dancing light into his eye. He considered the crowd for a moment, opened his mouth, and spoke.

"People of Lan Dinas." He bellowed the words, and was pleased to hear them ring in the air. He might not have the delivery of a professional speaker, but he was heard throughout the square. "You have come here tonight because of a threat. Our peaceful home, our sacred island, has been infected by a corrupting influence."

Cockram thought the opening a rather good one, but the people in the crowd began to shift and mutter. A man midway back in the square shouted, cupping his hands before his mouth to help his voice carry. "Where's the rector, then? You're just a barkeep."

The comment sparked the reservoir of Cockram's anger. He felt the hatred he'd carried since his sister's death rise up and surge through him, strengthening his voice.

"I am someone who has faced our foe and been scarred by the experience. I am someone who knows the truth. Six months ago, I was attacked by a tessila. It injured my leg, and it took my eye."

Since it had happened, Cockram had not shown his injury to anyone other than the sisters of Delari who had tended his wounds after Tilde told him, with unusual firmness, that he would die if he didn't go to the cloister for help. Now, he felt the heat of the torches, smelled their heavy smoke on the air and gazed out at the scared, restless people he needed to fuse into a mob. In a fit of inspiration, he reached up and snatched the eyepatch away, revealing the sunken eyelid the sisters had sewn shut. The stitches were gone now, but the lid had sealed itself, becoming a permanent, deflated flap.

As the faces in the crowd creased with fascinated disgust, Cockram told his story. He told the story his way. It was a narrative he'd rehearsed so many times, he'd have been hard pressed to tell the true tale if he'd wanted to.

When he was done, he had their attention. As he spoke his final words, the crowd was silent. No more muttering. No more shifting glances. Cockram could feel the energy of his narrative spilling out of him and into them. He concluded, "So she took an innocent child, and she made him into a monster. Like her. And then corrupted his father as well, for good measure."

At that moment, there was a disturbance in the crowd, a shifting of bodies to one side of the square. Cockram looked up to see the boy he'd sent for Dinon trying to shoulder his way back to the platform. Cockram called to him. "Here. Boy. Where's the rector?"

The boy stopped and raised his face. Cockram could see it was streaked with tears. His voice came out in a high, thin wail. "Dead. Rector Dinon is dead. Killed, no one knows how. There's not a mark on the body, the sisters say. It's like it was done by magic."

The streets were strangely deserted. Marim had left Embriem's house and turned left, descending the gentle rise towards the line of shops that stood near the lakeshore. She suspected there was a more direct path to the harbor. She'd seen various footpaths cut up the steeper slopes, but she hadn't been back to the docks since she'd arrived here, and the fog made it difficult to cut across country. She'd decided to play it safe and stay on the roads.

She walked quickly, Kix nestled in her cloak's collar, her sea bag slung over a shoulder. The thing was full to bursting and seemed to drag against her, pulling her back and down as if it didn't want her to go.

The fog was thick, and she had no light. She could have summoned a spell, but something about that strange glow in the sky over the town square, something about the way no one seemed to be about, cautioned her not to give herself away. She hurried, already out of breath before she reached the place Embriem had found her all those months ago. She paused to take stock of her surroundings.

In spite of living on this island for months, she'd rarely come into town. Oh, certainly, she'd passed through. She'd gone into the occasional shop, buying an odd thing or two she found herself in need of. On those outings, she always told herself she would try to be friendly, talk to some people she met on the road or offer to heal a wounded carthorse.

Somehow, though, she never had. The people she met seemed little inclined to engage with her, and she never came across an animal in need of her skills. Eventually, it had seemed easier just to stay in with Tassin.

Now, walking along the quiet, cobbled street, it seemed like such a waste. She looked at the tidy storefronts, the lamp lit windows. What did she have to show for her time here? Not a single friendship, that was for sure.

In the distance, she heard a muffled roar. She stopped, thinking at first a strange wind had risen and was catching in the eaves of the surrounding houses. But as she stood and strained to hear, she realized it was voices. Human voices raised in a collective bellow.

Fear washed over her. She couldn't say why, but Marim felt a sudden need to hide. She scampered off the road like a mouse feeling the vibrations of a stampeding carriage to hide herself behind a stack of crates next to the bakery. She eased her way between two piles, breathing in the scent of flour. Then, ears perked, she waited.

Kix stirred, moving to peep past the folds of her hood. She stilled him with a thought. He subsided grudgingly, made restless by her surging emotions.

A minute passed, then another. The roaring seemed to grow louder. The general hum of it separated into individual shouts, raised voices ringing with anger and excitement.

Then they were spilling past her hiding place – a veritable horde of men and women. They wore plain, rough clothing and carried torches. They streamed by in a rush, passed through the strip of shops, and turned. Their movement caught Kix's interest. He moved to fly out after them, to get a better look. "No," Marim hissed. "You stay put. Stay in my hood until we're on the ship. This is important, Kix." Her tessila subsided with ill grace, and Marim returned her attention to the crowd.

She didn't have a good view of the street. She could make out the passing people only through a small crack between two crates. Still, it wasn't hard to trace the route they were taking. They had turned, and were going uphill. She could hear their voices, see the smeared red light in the sky.

They're going for Embriem. The thought formed in her mind, solid and clear. But she pushed it aside. No. This couldn't have anything to do with her former employer. It was clearly some kind of worker's riot, some issue with low wages or long hours or some other conflict between rich and poor.

Still, she stayed behind her crates until the stragglers were well gone from view. Then, heart pounding, she crept back into the street, stopping at the corner to look both ways and make sure she wouldn't be seen.

She hesitated one more moment, looking back the way she'd come. She could still hear the crowd, still see the bobbing torches. But she couldn't really be sure which street they'd chosen. And even if they were heading for Embriem's, his affairs didn't concern her any longer.

With a quick heave, Marim shouldered her bag again and stepped out into the street.

Vailria stood on the deck of the ship, watching the moving lights in the town with a raised chin. Captain Tommin stood next to her, his blunt hands set on the railing. Together, they watched the light spill from the town square and begin to move through the streets. "You see," Vailria said. "It begins."

Captain Tommin was unhappy. He'd been thrilled to see her at first, hurrying up from his cabin the moment his mate brought word she'd come on board. She'd been waiting in the harbor for half the day, and had insisted on boarding the moment the gangplank was run out. She accepted the captain's chaste hug, his light kiss on her cheek, and his warm, rumbled greeting. Then she'd said, "You have to put out again. Immediately."

He'd drawn back from her, brow furrowed. He was a kind man – even-tempered and fair. It was one of the things that had drawn her to him in the first place. Now, his normally sunny expression clouded over. "Don't be ridiculous," he said. "I have cargo I've been hauling with me for over a year that will find a market here. I have a passenger to take up. And I want to spend some time with you." His tone softened towards the end of his speech, and he smiled.

She did not return the smile. She looked him in the eye. "I'm coming with you. I will not—cannot—wait any longer."

He blinked his gray eyes, the lightness draining out of his expression. He rubbed at his beard, eyeing her with sharpened interest.

Around them, the deck was a maelstrom of activity. Men were crawling up and down the riggings, furling the sails and shifting crates that were tethered to the deck. Vailria wanted to shout at them, to tell them to stop.

Down in the city, torches were dense in the town square. The feel of the air was ugly, the mood of the people scared and uncertain. Vailria hadn't expected to find Lan Dinas in such a state. She'd planned to go to the ship, spend a few days with the captain as he traded and took on supplies, to gradually talk him around to agreeing to her plan.

On her way through town that afternoon, however, Vailria had grown afraid. She'd stopped several times to eavesdrop on angry, muttered conversations. She heard the words "brinlin" and "Tessilari" in every one.

She'd gone back for Tok at that point. She'd not taken him with her, at first, thinking she'd have a few days to ferry anything she wanted with her onto the ship. On her way back through town, she saw the situation had degraded further. She'd kept to the shadows, hidden in a passive echo spell.

It took a while for Tommin to answer. She spoke again, to make certain he understood. "I need to leave this place. Now."

Tommin stepped away from her, leaning on the railing. "Are you in some kind of trouble?"

She looked at him, itching to put her hand on his arm, to persuade him with a little nudge of magic rather than a long argument. She resisted. "The town is on the verge of a riot. The harbor isn't safe. If the mob comes here, you could be looted. You could lose everything. You could be harmed or killed. Your ship, after all, is guided by magic."

Tommin stood straighter. That was when he saw the strange glow in the sky. He looked at her, mouth tight. "We haven't enough food and water to make it to Masidon. That's where we're headed next. I need to complete my route."

Vailria was shaking her head. "I can't go to Masidon. You know that. It's time for you to make good on your promise at last, to take me to this little island you've been talking about for the last ten years. Please," she continued as a group of men flung one of the holds open with a resounding thud, "tell your men to stop."

He looked at her for one more suspended instant and she knew, suddenly, it had all been a lie. All the years she'd waited, believing his promise they would one day have a life together, would come to nothing. None of it had been real. Or, at least, not real enough to count when she finally asked him to change.

Then a young man came careening down the road to the harbor. He stopped on the docks and bellowed his news to no one in particular. "The rector's dead. Murdered in his quarters. Killed by the Tessilari girl, they say. There's a mob gone to find her, to deliver justice."

Tommin sucked in a deep breath, turned and called out to his first mate, telling him to close the holds and prepare the ship to push back out to sea. He spoke in a tight, low voice. "The wind and tide that brought us in will work against us now, so we can't use sail. I'll have to use the guide globe to push us out. It will take us a goodly while to get properly underway, but we can leave the docks behind soon enough."

Relief coursed through Vailria, so great it nearly overwhelmed her. She lifted her face to the lurid sky and said with quiet sincerity, "Thank you, Tommin."

There was noise and light outside. Embriem could see bobbing torches, a whole line of them, through the windows of his office. He could hear the rumble and shouts of a crowd. Some inner part of him stirred, livened by worry. *They're coming for you,* it warned him. *Take Tassin. Take Tassin and go.*

He fancied it was Chalsia's voice. If she had been with him, he would have handled all this better. She always had a way of seeing the small parts of a large problem, of breaking it down into its components and addressing each one in its own way.

Embriem was aware his current problems were manifold. He knew part of the issue was his own mind, the strange sheen that seemed to vibrate through his head when he'd been away from Nel for too long. But what was he supposed to do? Take Tassin and set up a permanent camp down on the lake shore? How could he conduct business? How could he receive guests? It wasn't possible. Not if he expected to remain a respected member of society.

But then, if the crowd approaching up the drive, carrying torches and shouting, was any indication, it was perhaps too late to convince Lan Dinas he was neither an aberration nor a threat. In spite of his best efforts, all his meetings, all his trade talks, all his attempts to reassure everyone he was the same man he'd always been, he had failed. Chalsia would not have failed. He was as certain of that as he was of his eternal love for her.

There was a pounding on the front door. Loud and insistent, the knocking rang through the front hall. The torches were close outside the window now, gathered in a knot at the top of the circle drive. Embriem waited for footsteps, for the sound of Baret moving to answer the knock. He didn't hear the man's hard tread, but instead the light patter of small feet.

Tassin peeped around the door frame, his pale face worried. He didn't come into the room, rather stood staring towards the window with wide eyes. "Da?" His voice was small. "Baret and Secha and all the staff have gone. They all went out the back an hour ago. Secha kissed me on the forehead. She was crying and she said I should stay in my room until it was over. I didn't know what she meant but I did stay. I stayed there until I heard the knocking on the door."

The pounding came again, this time accompanied by a shout. Embriem looked at his son, but there was that slippery sheen on his mind. He couldn't seem to think. He couldn't seem to find any reason to get up, to go to the door, to try to reason with the mob outside.

Tassin turned and took a few cautious steps back into the hall. He looked so small, his body held straight and sharp with alert concern. He stared into the gloomy entryway. "Do you think they'll break it, Da? The door? If we don't answer it, I mean?"

Embriem turned back to the window. It was only a matter of time, he supposed, until one of them had the idea to throw a torch at the house. It would fall at the base of the stone wall, and maybe it would gutter out. But then another would follow the first, and another, and sooner or later the fire would catch on a dormant rose bush or a small pile of fallen leaves.

Get up. Go speak to them. They're not beyond reason yet. The voice in his head was urgent, but Embriem was certain he would collapse if he tried to stand. Still, he sat up a little, trying to fight the haze in his mind. "Tassin," he said. "Run. Go out the back like the servants did. Go to Vailria's house. She'll help you. I'm sure."

Tassin's answer was quick and hopeful. "What about Marim? She didn't leave with the servants."

Marim. Embriem remembered something about Marim. She'd been here not long ago, speaking to him much as Tassin was now. He searched for the information, and found it. "She said she was going to the harbor to take a ship back to Masidon."

Tassin turned to look at his father. The look on his face made Embriem rear back with shock. There was anger in his eyes, a sharp, furious expression that looked alien on his gentle features. The boy turned and ran.

He didn't run to the back of the house. He ran to the front door and flung it open.

Abruptly, Embriem found the strength to stand. He took a few steps across the office, then was overcome by a sensation of vertigo. He had to cling to the door frame. He heard shouts from outside, a voice demanding, "Where's the Tessilari girl, then? Send her out or we'll burn your house to the ground."

Tassin's small voice piped up, sure and clear over the rumble of the agitated crowd. "She's not here," he said. "She's leaving the island. She went to the harbor to catch a ship."

CHAPTER 6

The mob had a life of its own now. Cockram stood off to one side, eyepatch back in place. He watched with satisfaction as a burly man carrying a torch pounded on Embriem's front door. People jostled behind him, muttering and glaring. The city guard had disappeared, melting away as if by magic. Some had taken off their vests and hats and joined the mob. Others had simply decided they would not risk their lives trying to restore order.

Cockram expected Embriem to answer, to stand there and try to diffuse the crowd. Instead, the door was heaved open by a thin boy.

His appearance was so unexpected, it brought a momentary lull to shouts and cries. Cockram felt a stirring of unease. The mob was still gathering momentum. While it might be capable of killing a child at its most bloodthirsty, this boy was unlikely to be the first victim. Feeling his first tremor of uncertainty since the surge of anger sparked by the announcement of the rector's death, Cockram watched, his one eye narrowed.

The boy, when asked for Marim, answered in a high, clear tone. He said she wasn't there, she'd decided to leave. She was going to the harbor and intended to take a ship back to where she'd come from.

The mob was not a flexible thing. It was like a bucket of water spilled down a hillside. Once the motion started, it was difficult to direct, difficult to divert unless channels had been set up beforehand. Now, the crowd stirred with unease and discontent. They wanted the Tessilari girl, and they wanted her now. The report she intended to leave the island was confusing.

"He's lying," someone yelled. "Search the house."

"That's the child she corrupted," someone else put in. "He's as evil as she is."

A mutter of agreement greeted this comment. Cockram made a snap decision. Events would unfold here one way or another, but if the Tessilari girl made it to the harbor, she might escape. While Cockram regretted this child must be destroyed and even felt a passing pang of regret Embriem must die as well, the girl's demise was an event he had eagerly anticipated for months.

As Tassin tried to respond to the crowd's accusations, Cockram turned on his heel. He carried no torch, and all eyes were fixed ahead on the small figure in the open doorway. It was simple for Cockram to slip away.

He moved slowly at first, not wanting to attract attention. Soon he was out of the glow of the torches, the warm fog shrouding him in welcome anonymity.

He reached the end of the drive, passed out the open gate, and turned right. He continued up the lane for a short while, then left it in favor of the narrow track that cut up the hillside and lead almost straight to the Rooster's Comb.

It was a steep route. Cockram's leg was bright with pain, his empty eye socket throbbing, well before he reached the top. But he was immune to physical discomfort now. He was driven by something stronger, something more elemental. He heaved himself towards the harbor, step by step, until the rise fell off abruptly and turned into a descent. He reached the harbor road at last and looked about, squinting.

The only light came from the lamps on the moored luggers and barges, and those outside his own establishment, which Tilde must have lit. But it was enough for him to see a figure on the road: a small person walking towards him, a bulky bag slung over one shoulder. A person who'd gone still at his sudden appearance.

The Tessilari girl, at last.

For a moment, they faced each other. From the harbor came the heavy sound of lapping waves and the quiet toll of a ship's bell calling for immediate departure. Cockram registered this sound, and smiled. With one hand, he drew a short, curved blade from his belt. With the other, he reached into his jacket and wrapped his fingers around the slim, hard rod Dinon had given him: his secret weapon. He recalled the words written about this artifact in the Directive, and they thrilled him. He need only make contact with either the Tessilari or her creature, and he would win.

After his first time touching the thing, Cockram only handled it with gloves. In preparation for this meeting, he'd slipped his hands into soft leather gauntlets the moment the mob left the square. Now, he was ready. He felt the familiar throbbing in his leg and in his head. More than anything, he wanted Marim's scaled beast to come after him again, to try to take him down. He would delight in stunning the creature, then stabbing it through the heart.

It didn't happen as he hoped. The girl paused for a moment like a frightened deer. Then, in a burst of movement, she began to run. She didn't run away from him, like he had expected. She ran towards him, trying to dodge her way past him on the road.

Cockram stepped to the side to block her. Heart thrilling, blood singing with anticipation, he crouched as she ran. She was near now. There was no sign of her creature. He raised the wand, preparing to strike a blow across her shoulder as she darted by.

She threw the sea bag at him. It was an ungainly, heavy thing, and it took him full in the chest. Cockram staggered, grunting, his blow deflected. The girl, light on her feet now, got her momentum beneath her and ran with the speed of the hunted.

With a bellow of rage, Cockram stumbled on his bad leg. The sea bag fell to the ground with a heavy thud. He turned, took a few strides in pursuit, then stopped dead in his tracks.

There was someone else on the road now, a figure draped in a cloak and wielding a staff. The newcomer was only a few paces away, positioned directly between Cockram and the fleeing girl.

His eye began to water and he felt a strange, lifting sensation in his head. He knew—knew without a doubt—this person had not been there a moment before.

His sense of triumph fading into fear, Cockram wiped his eye and stared as the figure raised one shapely arm, pale in the glowing fog, and pulled back her hood.

He recognized the face. How could he not? He'd seen it every day of his boyhood, and in every nightmare that had disturbed his sleep since.

She was no longer a child, of course. The energetic innocence he remembered was gone from her face. Her eyes, which had once looked on him with trust and love, now bore into him with sharp, glittering hatred.

She spoke. The sound of her voice pried at the fissures in his battered, hardened, heart. "Well, brother. It turns out you have a second chance to try to kill me." She whirled the staff in her hands, and grinned.

Braven followed the map. The pulsing dot led him upwards, onto a dirt track that ended in a cobbled street. He walked through the gathering dusk, keeping to the edge of the road.

There was a scent of acrid smoke on the air and a worrisome glow in the sky. He thought of Adni's words. *I'm going to kill the rector.* He had accepted her statement, let her go off to do murder.

Now, he wondered why he hadn't tried to stop her. Was watching her walk away, knowing her plans, any better than casting a spell that ended a man's life? Or kidnapping a child, for that matter?

He moved past a street lined in shops and up a roadway with large houses standing in isolated splendor. As he moved further away from the warmlake, the warmth faded from the air. Tendrils of mist stroked his face with cool fingers. He shivered.

The smell of smoke grew stronger. At last, he drew up to a massive gate standing open in a tall wall. He stopped, pulling his cloak in and hoping the passive echo spell knitted into its fabric worked as well as Adni had promised. In the distance, beyond the gate, he could see a large house. All over its front lawn and gardens stood people.

They were angry people. Braven could see that at a glance. They carried smoking, reeking torches and glared towards the towering house at the top of the drive. Nevertheless, they were strangely quiet. They had pulled together and were all staring at a figure that stood on the stoop.

Braven glanced down at his map, then shoved it into his pocket. No surprise, this was the house he needed. Adni hadn't mentioned dealing with a mob. He would have to go around the back.

Braven stepped off the road and sidled through the gate. Squinting against the glare of the torches, he moved up the wall, skirting the grounds, planning to swing around the back of the house and find a way in from behind.

He was nearly even with the front of the house when he heard a murmur ripple through the assembled crowd. He turned. For the first time, he registered how small the figure on the stoop really was. It was a child that stood there, addressing this mob. Braven caught the sound of his piping voice on the air, speaking in a high but somehow assured voice.

Braven stopped. He couldn't quite catch the words. He was too far away, and the voice didn't carry well. He took a few steps away from the wall, feeling suddenly he very much wanted to hear what the child had to say. The other people seemed to feel the same way. They were drawing in closer, faces raised, expressions rapt.

Braven took a step forward, then another. The breeze shifted and he caught a snatch of the boy's story. "… would have died, because our bodies changed. We didn't do it …"

It was Gia who made him realize what was happening. She stirred in his sleeve, uncoiling to release an angry hiss. It was then Braven recognized what he was feeling.

There was a prickle of magic on the air. It was radiating out over the mob, coming directly from the boy. It was falling down over the crowd in lazy loops, lulling them as he spoke.

With a sharp twist, Braven pulled his own mind away, throwing up a barrier between him and the magic that drifted with the fog on the air. As he did this, the boy's words cut off sharply. The tousled head jerked towards Braven, as if he'd felt the spell that had interfered with his own casting.

Adni's voice came back to him. *His name is Tassin. He and his father are brinlings.* This had to be the boy she'd sent him to collect.

The crowd shifted, a ripple of restlessness coursing through the gathered people as the boy's spell flagged. Taking in the sheer number of bodies and torches, Braven made a split-second decision. He let go of his shield, letting his own weaving disperse on the smoke and fog laced air. Then he reached out for the boy's magic, found it, and closed his eyes.

Braven wasn't experienced with collaborative casting. Most of his time in the forest was spent alone. Now, he tried to gather the feel of the boy's spell. It was an ingenious little weaving, directed primarily at the feelings of anger and hatred, targeting those emotions and using them to bring about a stillness in the crowd. The method was a bit unorthodox, but it seemed to be effective. The trouble wasn't the concept behind the boy's work, it was his lack of power. He was very young, after all, and couldn't have been in his bond for long.

But Braven had plenty of power. As he gained an understanding of the spell that was soothing the crowd, he drew on his own connection with Gia. She was there with him, fresh from many days of basking in the waters of the warmlake. She had power to spare. He drew on it, pouring his own reserves into the boy's spell.

The child's voice faltered and he went still, transfixed by the sensation of Braven's working. It didn't matter. Words were no

longer needed. All around him, the people went still. Men stood
with torches raised, women huddled in their cloaks, all of them
suddenly as immobile as statues.

Braven, suddenly energized, darted forward and skirted the
crowd to leap up onto the stoop. He looked down at the boy, who
was staring at the frozen faces of those he'd bewitched. "Come
on," Braven said. "We have to go."

Marim pelted down the final stretch of road to the ocean. She
could hear the slap of the waves on the wharf and smell the tang of
the sea. She ran, unencumbered by her bag, Kix clinging to the
inside of her hood and annoyed by the rough ride.

She heard no sound of pursuit. Slowing to glance back over
her shoulder, she stumbled to a halt.

She could see the man who had tried to stop her. Cockram,
his name was. She'd met him once, down by the warmlake not
long after she arrived on Cynnes Tarth. He was different now. She
remembered him as friendly and good looking. But he'd somehow
lost an eye since then, and the look on his face when he'd stepped
into the road could only be described as ugly.

He stood still now, feet planted, her sea bag lying a short
distance behind him.

But he wasn't alone. Another person stood between Marim
and Cockram – a person wearing a long cloak that seemed to shift

and blur in the swirling fog. For a moment, Marim thought it must be Vailria. But this person was a little too short, a little too sturdy, and she was wielding a staff with an ease that reminded Marim of some of the Tessilari.

Marim hesitated, anxious and confused. Why was Cockram here? Why had he placed himself between Marim and the harbor? Why had the sight of him filled her with so much fear she'd run from him on pure reflex?

Even as she wondered, she felt the tantalizing tickle of memory shifting beneath the surface of her mind. She seemed to hear Cockram's voice speaking in the fog as she walked with Tassin clutched to her chest. *Can I help in some way? Carry the boy, perhaps?*

She paused, arrested by the muddled memories. She'd never been able to fully recall what had happened the day Embriem and Tassin found their brinlins, the day Kix had shifted for the first time. Neither had Embriem or Tassin. Marim now understood part of this had been Vailria's interference, but most of it was to do with overextension, the effects of the magic she must have used to get Embriem out of the house and Tassin down to the lake.

It had bothered her from time to time, but until now it had never seemed particularly significant. Now, as terror and confusion warred with the maddening sensation of having forgotten something important, she wished she'd talked to Embriem about that day when she'd had the chance.

Squinting into the fog, Marim became aware of Kix. Her tessila was thrilling with a deep, violent rage. With a start, she realized he wanted to go back and attack Cockram. He was keeping to her directive not to leave her hood until they reached the ship only with a great deal of difficulty.

Kix took his eye. The thought surfaced, wavered, and Marim's confusion multiplied. Before she could sort it out, before she could impose any kind of sense on her own muddled memories, she heard the single peal of the harbor bell that announced the departure of a merchant vessel.

More agitated than ever, Marim wheeled and began to run again. As she careened down to the wharf, she tried to reassure herself. It must be another ship leaving – a different one.

Even as she told herself this, Marim felt her stomach twist with fear. She knew not many ships came into the harbor here. There were a multitude of the lighter, smaller vessels used for trade between the islands, but a true ship, one that could survive the Two Trials and reach Masidon, was rare. Only two had docked in the six months Marim had lived here, both recently come from Masidon with no plans to return until they'd made a circuit of the other islands.

Marim remembered how unhappy the crew had been to have her aboard by the end. She remembered Captain Tommin's kind eyes, his promise he would come back for her to carry her home on his return voyage. She'd heard the first bell announcing the ship's arrival only a short time ago. Why would he write? Why would he dock only to immediately put back to sea without her?

Her mind abuzz with too many questions, Marim stumbled at last onto the stone quay. It was not difficult to spot Captain Tommin's vessel. It towered over the flat barges and light sailboats tied up to the surrounding docks, its many masts reaching into the darkening sky.

The fog was restless over the water. Marim came to a halt before the rearing wall of the ship's massive hull. She stared up, trying to pick out some detail that would tell her if the ship was leaving or not. She could see activity on deck, sailors moving crates, tying or untying ropes. When she'd been on board, Marim had never been able to find any order in the constant movement that happened on the deck.

Breathing heavily, Kix still hunched, seething, in her hood, Marim stared into the fog. She looked for a gangplank and saw none. She squinted harder, staring at the hull and its position against the jetty. As she watched, she saw with dismay the ship was creeping backwards. Inch by inch, it was moving away from her, putting out to sea.

Marim waved her arms. The sunset was gone now, its bloom faded to the last light before dark. But the dock was well lit, as was the ship's deck. She raised her voice and shouted, knowing she would never be heard above the slap of the water and the groaning of the ship's timbers. She tried anyway. "Captain Tommin." Her voice seemed weak and breathless in the heavy air. "Captain Tommin. Please. You promised. Wait!"

As she yelled, craning her neck to see past the prow that towered in front of her, Marim noticed two figures standing at the railing. One was a burly form recognizable by his distinctive hat. Captain Tommin turned his face in her direction as she shouted, as if he'd somehow heard her. Hope surged through Marim's veins like fire.

But then she recognized the other figure. A slender woman, dressed in a plain woolen gown with a high collar.

Vailria.

The hope died as Marim understood. Vailria had gotten aboard somehow and compelled the captain to leave Marim behind.

But why? She remembered Vailria now, their bitter exchange in Embriem's sitting room, but she didn't understand. Marim thought the woman would have been glad to see her leave Cynnes Tarth.

Too confused now to do anything but stare, Marim let her arms fall to her sides. The captain looked down, an expression of regret on his face. Vailria's features were a mask of cool reserve, her thoughts and emotions unreadable.

Marim stood there, a chill creeping over her as she tracked the ship's slow backwards progress. As she watched, Vailria set her hand on the captain's arm. The two of them turned away from the railing and disappeared from view.

Ever since she learned the truth from Old Mino, Adni had dreamed of this moment: of looking into her brother's eyes and seeing understanding slowly dawn in his face. He'd been an intelligent boy, resourceful and quick. All these years, he thought he'd pulled it off. He believed he'd succeeded in orchestrating his sister's death.

Now, as she stood between Cockram and the Tessilari girl he'd taken to hunting as ruthlessly as he'd once hunted her, Adni felt giddy with the rush of revealing herself at last. He had only one eye now, but the shock and horror he felt was plain enough to see. Adni savored the moment, just standing there, allowing him to absorb her presence, letting it sink into his psyche like blood spilling into sand.

She twirled her staff in her hands. Behind her, the girl's running steps faded. Cockram's face was bloodless and horrified, his one eye staring as if he was sure she was a ghost. She set the butt of her staff on the ground again, and waited.

Cockram blinked and glanced around, but they were alone. There were men on the docks further down, and Cockram's own daughter in the Rooster's Comb just ahead. But with the light fading and the fog thick around them, they might as well have been the only two people on the island.

At last, Cockram found his voice. It came out choked, as if his throat was constricted or dry. "Adni."

That was all he said. That single word, her name, spoken as he'd said it when they were children and they'd gotten themselves into some sort of scrape. It cut at her, seeming to reach past all the hardness she'd built up, hitting a tender, unguarded place in her heart. As if to punctuate the word, the harbor bell gave a single, resonant toll.

For a moment, she felt her resolve falter. While she hesitated, she saw Cockram begin to recover. He drew in a breath, shook his head, and spoke again, his voice firmer now. "Adni. What miracle is this? Delari be praised. We thought you dead." He took a step forward.

It was too much, too effusive, too quick. She knew him too well to be drawn in. She could read the calculations churning behind that one eye. He was spinning the situation, twisting the truth. He wasn't happy to see her. He was only adapting, testing, looking for the best path forward.

The soft spot on her heart hardened over.

Sure of herself again, Adni spoke in a quiet, measured tone, ignoring Cockram's outpouring and raising the staff to warn him not to come any closer. "Dinon is dead."

Overhead, seagulls flew, their lonely voices muffled on the foggy air. She watched her brother's face as she spoke, but the news was not a shock. He only gave a quick nod. He'd already heard then, which was all to the good. She added with a thin smile, "Dead by my hand."

That didn't shock him either. He was quick, her brother. He'd already guessed as much, already connected her return with the news from the cloister. But he wasn't through playing, hadn't given up on trying to find an advantage. He managed to look confused. His voice was gentle as he answered, as if he thought her feverish or hysterical. "I'm told it was done by magic. It couldn't have been you."

Adni looked at him, feeling the echo of a sort of fondness. *Oh my brother,* she thought. *You always were such a good liar.*

Behind Cockram, on the path back down to the city, Adni saw the bulk of the large sea bag the girl had been carrying. It had been lying where it had fallen, an inert, humped shape in the fading light. Now, oddly, it shifted, rolled partway over, and lifted into the air. Once off the ground, it disappeared.

The sight was so arresting, Adni was momentarily distracted. She stared at the place in the air where the bag had hovered for a fraction of a second. Then she tore her gaze away, bringing her eyes to settle again on her brother's face.

But he was too quick. He'd seen her attention shift. He spun around and stood gazing at the empty road behind him. She saw him register the missing bag, saw him understand. He spoke to the air, his voice contemptuous. "Missed your ship, did you Tessilari? Where will you go now? There's a mob outside of Embriem's house, you know. They'll probably kill him and the boy. But do you know what they're really hunting? You."

He laughed. It was a mad sound. He set out at a walk down the road as if he'd forgotten Adni's existence. Anger shot through her in a hot bolt.

Even after all this time, even with the shock she'd given him, she was nothing to him. He'd rather continue his hunt than stand and face her.

Adni found herself reaching for the blow gun.

But, no. She stopped herself. She had decided when she set out tonight that her brother's death would not be easy or simple. They needed to finish their conversation before she killed him. She needed him to understand how thoroughly she had won.

She snatched her hand away from the weapon and began to jog, intending to get ahead of Cockram and force him to face her again. But he darted off the road and took a side path that descended, hard and fast, towards Lan Dinas below.

He was familiar with the track, and she was not. The light from the harbor fell behind. Adni found herself plunging downwards through the fog and the gathering dark. She schooled herself into a rhythm, narrowing her focus to the lumpy path, her footfalls, and the dim blur of Cockram's white shirt ahead in the fog.

Then the path leveled out, and she saw the smear of torches on the night. She had to stop suddenly to avoid running full into her brother, who had stopped at the edge of a crowd drawn up in front of a large house.

The crowd was large enough to fill the entire space between the building and the road. The people stood close together, many of them holding torches. And they all stood strangely still, all gazing at the stoop as if it held the answer to their prayers.

But the house was dark, the stoop empty. Adni felt a prickle of understanding. Braven must have been here. He must have done something to bewitch all these people. Everyone always said he was strong, but this show of power surprised her.

Adni was still taking in the arresting sight of the frozen crowd when Cockram wheeled on her suddenly, striking out with a small, silver rod he held in his hand.

Marim turned away from the ship with one thought at the forefront of her mind. Her sea bag. Back up on the street, it had seemed worth it to ditch her baggage if it meant escaping from Cockram and reaching the ship. She carried her purse on her belt and wore one of her two stitchrings around her neck. None of her other belongings were strictly essential to her survival.

As soon as she realized she wasn't, in fact, going to sail for Masidon, Marim thought frantically of her tablets. They were her one connection to home, her only means of communicating with the Tessilari. Her spellbook, too, was in there – more invaluable than ever if she intended to go into hiding in the forest.

Still breathless from her dash down to the harbor, Marim jogged back up the slope. Cresting the rise, she saw Cockram and the strange, cloaked figure. They appeared to be having a conversation. Her bag was visible behind the man, a lump in the road. *This would be so easy for any of my friends.* The thought was bitter. Marim herself had never managed a fully successful passive echo spell.

Standing at the edge of the road, Marim hesitated. Kix was still in her hood, chafing with a desire to fly. It was remarkable, how well he was containing himself.

The thought made Marim remember in a sudden rush. She had changed. Not all Tessilari were capable of casting the same spells. Most had strengths and weaknesses. Before, Marim had only had weaknesses. But now was no time to be inhibited by the past.

She had changed. Kix was better. Any graduate of the academy should be able to cast and hold a passive echo spell, at least for a short while.

"Don't think. Just do." She muttered the words under her breath, and began her weaving.

It was slow at first. She had to fumble after the spell, trying to recall her old lessons. She seemed to hear Professor Liam's voice in her head. *The key to the passive spells is their structure – the baseline of energy you use to support them.*

It came to her then, the logic behind the weave she had begun so many times but failed to complete. She flew through the rest of the spell, tied it off, and dropped it over herself. She could feel it snug around her, the way it displaced the energy of the air and the fog. It would keep people from noticing her unless she drew their attention.

And the fog was a help. Feeling sudden hope, Marim hurried forward. She left the road to skirt Cockram and the woman, then returned to it once she'd moved by. Her heart was pounding as she crept out of the verge, approached her sea bag, picked it up, and pushed on her weaving until it encompassed both her and the ungainly object.

Marim was so relieved to have her things back in her possession, she didn't realize her mistake until Cockram turned around, eyes vivid with anger.

Stupid, stupid, Marim berated herself. What had she been thinking? Of course, the woman would have noticed the large bag seemingly levitate and then blink out of existence.

Cockram wheeled, turning away from the woman in the cloak to sweep the street for Marim. She felt the stirring of fear again, mixed with Kix's desire to kill. Together, the emotions were nearly overwhelming. *I should run.* The thought came to her, but without much force. She only stood in place, the passive echo spell snug around her, the sea bag heavy on her shoulder.

Cockram spoke, addressing the dark lane at large since he couldn't see her. "Missed your ship, did you Tessilari? Where will you go now? There's a mob outside of Embriem's house, you know. They'll probably kill him and the boy. But do you know what they're really hunting? You."

The words filled her with the old creeping blend of rage and horror. *No matter what I do, where I go,* she thought, *I bring disaster down on those around me.*

She remembered the mob, the angry muttering, the torches. She'd convinced herself they weren't after Embriem.

And she'd been right. They were after her.

She stood in the darkness, trembling. Cockram laughed. Before she could decide what to do, he was walking away, heading for a path that left the road.

He knew what she hadn't yet admitted to herself.

There was only one place for Marim to go. Mob or no mob, she had to go back to Embriem's.

CHAPTER 7

In the 30 years that had passed between Adni's funeral and this moment, Cockram had never once found a way to believe she might still be alive. He had been there, after all. He'd stood in the front hall as the death procession entered his house. He'd been deemed too young to attend the ceremony, so he'd sat alone in the cold front room, and waited. It hadn't taken long. Soon, the sisters were back again, moving in their double line out the front door of the small hut.

He'd heard the high, keening sound of his mother's wails. He'd crept into the hall and looked around the door frame. He'd seen the rector there, standing over the bent form of his mother. He'd seen the narrow shape of his sister in her bed.

And after that, he didn't remember anything, really. Had there been a funeral? He couldn't recall. He didn't remember her body being moved, or the rector leaving. All he remembered of the days that followed was his mother's grief and his own need to escape from it.

It was strange, now that he thought about it. He remembered telling those few who'd asked the funeral had been small. Private. But why couldn't he remember the ceremony? Surely, at least he and his mother had stood beside the grave and seen Adni lowered in. There was a little stone in the cemetery with Adni's name on it. His mother had kept flowers blooming there all through the summer months until the day she died.

So how could it be his sister, now, who emerged out of the fog to thwart him when he was about to have his revenge?

At first, he suspected a trick – some twisted magic taking the form of someone he'd lost. But how could any spell have known exactly the way his sister spoke, the way she moved, the way she cocked her head when she was annoyed? How could it have divined exactly what 30 years of age would do to the child Cockram remembered?

It was impossible. Even less possible than the chance Adni had not died. After all, he'd heard the stories. The night the death procession had come for Tassin, the Tessilari girl had snatched him right out from under the rector's nose.

Perhaps Adni had somehow feigned death. In any case, it didn't matter. If Adni was alive, it meant she was one of *them* now. It meant she'd used magic to twist his mind, muddling his memories of what had happened. It meant she had a bond with the creature she'd found in the lake.

It meant she needed to die as surely as the Tessilari girl did.

Running down the slope, heading back the way he'd come, Cockram came to a decision. As much as his sister's sudden arrival had startled him, as much as he wished he could go back in time and save her, set her feet on a different path than the one she'd chosen, nothing had changed. His sister might be alive in the flesh, but she was dead in spirit. She'd chosen to divide her soul. As long as she lived, she would be nothing more than an abomination. The best gift he could give her was freedom from her own cursed existence.

So, Cockram must simply do again what he'd done before. And he'd have to manage it alone this time.

Cockram reached the street and dashed through the gates into the drive before Embriem's house. He had half a moment to pause, to take in the strange stillness of the crowd, before he heard Adni pull up behind him. He smiled to himself. He didn't doubt she was faster than he was. She could have struck him in the back or clubbed him over the head, but she hadn't. Which meant, despite her bravado, she didn't really want to harm him. That would give him the advantage.

As she came to a stop, he whirled, lashing out with Dinon's rod. He didn't need to land a hard blow. All he needed was to touch her. He expected it to be easy.

But Adni surprised him. As he spun, she danced back out of range, countering immediately with a deft whirl of her staff. She cracked the staff against the rod in his gloved hand.

The blow was hard. Cockram cursed as his fingers went numb. He staggered back, shaking his hand, the rod falling from his grasp. Behind him, the crowd was strangely silent, but as Adni pressed forward, staff whirling, a few at the edge of the crowd turned to stare vaguely towards the sounds of conflict.

Adni was strangely difficult to focus on, her body shifting and blurring as she moved. The staff sliced through the air as it arced down toward Cockram's head. He stumbled back, feeling the rush of wind as the engraved shaft of the weapon whistled past his ear. Cursing, he tried to center himself, tried to come up with a strategy.

But the rod was gone. It had fallen to the ground and rolled off somewhere. The fog was thick. Full dark had fallen. He glanced around, but the flaring torches stabbed his eye, making him blind. He could see no sign of the weapon. He was on the defensive with nothing but his short blade to block that whirling, snapping, staff.

The staff came again. He blocked the swing, but a shudder of energy ran up the blade of his weapon, cracking against his palm with a shock of resounding force. He cried out and dropped his sword.

Suddenly, he was unarmed.

Behind him, Cockram heard muttering. Adni raised her voice, shouting loud enough to be heard at the edges of the crowd. "This man's a liar," she said. "And a murderer. I'm his sister, Adni. He tried to kill me when we were children. Now, he's killed the rector and has turned you all against the people who live here to divert attention from what he really is."

She swung the staff as she spoke. Cockram tried to back away, but he bumped into the rustling hedge that lined the drive. Adni's staff was in motion. The blow was going to fall, and he had no way to protect himself.

As often happened in high stakes moments, Cockram's senses seemed to sharpen. Time seemed to slow down. He became aware of everything around him. He smelled the green scent of the leaves he'd crushed when he stumbled into the hedge, overlaid by the tarry stink of the torches.

He raised his arm above his head, his only hope of warding off the falling staff. As he did, he saw Adni's other arm. It blurred, dipping towards her belt and pulling out a throwing dagger.

He saw her intention. While he blocked the blow to his head, she was going to knife him in the gut.

More people in the crowd were stirring now, turning to regard the commotion with strangely blank faces. But no one moved to help.

He was out of time.

The staff hit Cockram's raised forearm. He felt the staggering force of it, felt the bone in his arm crack. He cried out even as Adni whipped the knife free and dove forward.

He did something, then, because he had no choice. He called on the secret piece of himself he'd hidden his entire life – the part that attracted him to the warmlake, that made him want to wade into the water and stand there, staring at the brinlins until one of them came to him and set its tiny webbed toes on his outstretched fingers.

He'd never forgotten the day Adni had shown him her brinlin – the way she'd uncurled her fingers and revealed the tiny, perfect creature that sat on her palm. He'd felt awe first. Then jealousy. Then anger.

It wasn't fair. Cockram had done as he'd been told. He'd stayed away from the warmlake, resisted its beckoning call. He'd stayed with his mother most days, helping her with the chickens and pigs, running deliveries and messages while Adni roamed about the island at will, doing whatever she wanted, getting a brinlin for her very own.

He'd tried to touch her brinlin. He'd reached out with a tentative finger, curious what that brilliant hide felt like. But the creature had drawn back, hissing, and Adni had snatched her hand away. "Don't," she'd said. "He's mine."

Now, all these years later, he remembered the sting of that rejection. The pain in his arm, the anger he'd been carrying since he lost his eye, the terrible truth that Adni, after all, had survived, all combined in him and gathered in that secret space.

Cockram felt something come alive inside him. It seemed to uncurl and somehow spark against the rooster pin in his scarf.

The knife was flying now, and Adni was looking at him, her eyes wicked and satisfied.

He did something. He had no idea what. He drew on the living thing inside himself and slashed at the knife in the air.

A blue wall of light flashed into existence, flaring forth through the pin and into the world. It encased Cockram as if in a dome of pure energy.

The knife hit the wall, threw up a shower of sparks, and fell harmlessly to the earth.

Cockram looked to Adni. He expected to see rage in her eyes, the fury of the thwarted.

Instead, she was smiling.

She addressed the gathered crowd again. "Here's your abomination, people of Lan Dinas." With that, she pulled up the hood of her cloak, turned, and disappeared into the mist.

Marim reached the bottom of the path and stepped out onto Embriem's street. She glanced back bitterly, wondering if she'd have reached the ship in time if she'd only known about this path earlier in the day. But then all thoughts of ships and shortcuts left her mind when she looked ahead and saw the mob in front of Embriem's house.

Cockram and the woman had re-engaged, and Marim saw her chance. She set out at a brisk jog, darting through the gate. She continued past the mob, around the side of the house, and made her way to the back door via the garden path.

The door, she found, was not locked. She set her hand on the latch and felt it click. It swung inward on its heavy hinges. Inside, the hallway was dark. No one had lit the lamps.

Up until this moment, Marim hadn't had a plan. Now, she set her bag down with a thump. She considered her situation. Embriem had refused to go with her once, but that was before a mob had gathered before his house, carrying torches.

Groping her way down the hall, Marim heard voices ahead. She recognized Tassin's piping tones and thought it must be Embriem answering him. But then she made it out the mouth of the dark hall and came into the entryway.

The lamps weren't lit there either, but she could make out three figures before the large windows that looked out over the front drive. Beyond them, the flames of the torches danced in the night.

Tassin was speaking, his voice carrying an odd, strained note Marim had never heard in it before. "… outside are angry. Braven knows a safe place. It's called Gol Ledrith. He's going to take us there."

Embriem's voice came back, harsh and hollow. Marim could make out her former employer now. He was standing strangely, huddled against the wall with his arms folded across his chest. "No." His voice was frantic and confused. "I won't leave her. There is hope." He'd deteriorated further even since she'd left.

The third figure turned then, becoming aware of Marim's presence. Backlit by the window, she could make out only the outline of his form. He was a sturdy man, shorter than Embriem but broader across the shoulders. He wore a cloak, thrown open to hang behind him.

Sensing alarm in the way he spun around, Marim spoke pre-emptively. "It's ok. I'm a friend."

At the sound of her voice, Tassin wheeled, stared for a heartbeat, and ran towards her. He hit her a little hard, making her stagger, and then he was clinging to her, crying. "Marim. Da said you'd gone. He said you'd gone and weren't coming back."

Kix, ever jealous, decided returning to the house amounted to same thing as reaching the ship. He squirmed out from within Marim's hood and took flight at last. He flitted about her head and landed on her arm, hissing. Marim shushed him, but she heard a sharp intake of breath from the strange man. She felt a strange constriction in her heart, and said in as soothing a voice as she could manage. "I haven't left, Tassin. I'm here."

She set a hand on the boy's shoulder and was visited by a sudden memory of Coll – the way he'd always felt so thin through his nightclothes when he climbed into bed with her.

The stranger spoke, his voice a little awed. "Is the boy telling the truth? You are Tessilari?"

Outside, the torches seemed to be growing more active. Whatever strange spell had lain over the crowd when she'd crept by was losing its hold.

"Yes."

Marim had intended to go on, to elaborate slightly about her limitations, but the man gave her no time. "Thank the tides," he said. Then he added, "Take this, can you? I'll deal with the father."

Marim's eyes had adjusted to the dark. She could make out the hint of the man's features, regular and smooth, but he didn't seem to be handing her anything. She stared for a moment, confused. Then she felt a little tug of magic. She realized he was offering her a spell.

She opened herself to his weaving. As it came into focus, a little gasp of astonishment escaped her. It was a massive thing, bigger than any she'd ever known of. It extended out over the crowd like an umbrella, locking the people in their strange stillness. "How did you do that?"

The man shrugged. "It's the boy's work. I only helped. But I can't persuade this one to go with us and keep it up at the same time."

Marim tried to take the spell, but it was no use. She couldn't grip the magic. Just like the times she'd tried to pass active threads to Tassin, it didn't work. After a few attempts, she shook her head. "It's no good," she explained. "We're too different."

The man stood a moment, looking troubled. "We'll have to leave him then, unless you can persuade him. We can't physically force him, and if I let go of this lot now, they'll be through this door and hard on our heels. I can't allow anyone to follow us."

Tassin, hearing the words, let go of Marim and turned with a wail to fling himself at his father. Marim felt the spell waver and dip, shifting and shimmering as the boy's agitation interfered with his ability to hold it in place. "Easy," the man said. "Tassin, easy. Stay focused now."

But Tassin was clinging to Embriem's hand, sobbing and tugging. "Please Da." His tone was heart-rending. "Please come." But Embriem, face blank, only braced against the pulls like a piqued mule.

The crowd outside rippled again. As a pounding sounded on the front door, she stepped forward and set her hand on Embriem's arm. A flutter of déjà vu passed over her, the strange sensation this had happened before.

Marim didn't know where she found the strength or the knowledge. Tessilari skilled in mindwork were rare, and Marim herself had little experience with persuasion.

She shouldered her confusion aside, drew as much power through her bond as she could get ahold of, and spoke in a firm, calm voice. "Come with me, Embriem. Now."

Braven felt the spell. Hard and sharp, it leapt into existence and wrapped itself around the boy's farther. The man jerked upright like a puppet snapped alive on its strings, his eyes wide and staring.

"Come with me," the girl repeated. Then she turned back to Braven. "I'm Marim," she said. "I take it you're a …" she broke off and made a vague gesture towards Tassin. "I take it you're like him?"

The girl, Tessilari though she was, had a smooth, young face and wide eyes, with her hair cut short in a way that accentuated her sharp features and struck Braven as pleasing and exotic. She was several inches shorter than he was, and slim. Her shoulders seemed narrow within her bulky cloak. Her tessila was a sinuous, spikey thing, with sharp wings and glittering eyes and a way of leaping into the air and landing again that Gia found unsettling.

"Braven," he said with a nod. "I'm Braven and yes, I'm a Brinlock. I've been sent to get you out of here before the people out there turn murderous." He glanced at Embriem, who had stood bolt upright and was now staring at Marim with a glazed look that made Braven uncomfortable.

The knocking sounded on the door again. Braven felt the restless people outside, pushing against the calming spell. He heard a voice drifting through the door, some words muffled, some clear. "… show you … not me … corruption …"

Tassin let out a strange whimper. He squeezed his eyes shut. "I can't hold it. I can't keep holding it."

Braven began to move. "Come on." He spoke the words with all the authority he could muster and headed towards the back of the house. There was a brief pause in the hall as Marim picked up a bulky sea bag and heaved it over her shoulder. Then, at last, they were out of the house and into the night.

In the darkness, shouts drifted on the foggy air. Braven pulled his cloak in, looking hopelessly at the garden paths. He didn't know the lay of the land from this point, didn't know if the wall went all the way around the property, or if they would need to pass the mob. He spoke to Tassin. "Can you get us to the warmlake? Not using any roads?"

As the boy nodded, Braven wondered about Adni. Was she out there, killing as she'd said she would? Would she ever come back to Gol Ledrith? Would he ever know what became of her?

They hurried away from the house, three people moving as individuals and a fourth that followed them in the jerky, spastic movements of the possessed. Braven tried not to think about that. Given the circumstances, he told himself, it was better than leaving the man behind.

He held the spell as long as he could, and felt the boy next to him doing the same. But at last, they were too far away.

He felt Tassin let go. The magic that had calmed the crowd unraveled and dispersed into the night.

Braven spoke into the fog. "Let's run for a while."

Adni melted into the shadows. Her plan, initially, was to discredit her brother, then kill him. But she'd decided during their confrontation that this was better than seeing him die by her own hand. It was better she leave him alive, better to use him as a scapegoat for the riot he'd started. The angry mob would have its way with him, and the original targets would slip away, unnoticed.

At least, that was what she hoped. She could feel Braven's spell over the crowd, doing something to sooth the violent emotions Cockram had roused in these people. She could also feel it failing – unraveling at the edges and beginning to disperse. "Get out of there," she muttered as she drew back into the fog to watch her brother face the consequences of what he'd done.

It wasn't unheard of, of course, for a person who had not actually bonded with a brinlin to manifest magical ability. Such a one's power was minimal, of course, but plenty a child in Gol Ledrith cast her first spell well before she grew acquainted with a brinlin. She'd always suspected her brother had such a latent power. He'd been too adamant in his hatred of the warmlake. She remembered the way she'd used to try to coax him to go with her to its shores, the way he would refuse as if he was better than she was because he could resist the pull, and she couldn't.

Couldn't. Or wouldn't. Adni hadn't tried. Now, as she watched the crowd begin to stir, brought slowly back to life by her brother's luminous spell and her own pronouncement, she thought she'd won.

She should have known better. As the crowd began to murmur and shift, Cockram raised his voice in a shout. The shield around him disappeared. He sprang towards the door of the mansion, his limp visible. "It's not me," he shouted. "It's them. It's the people inside this house. Follow me. I'll show you."

He barreled towards the door, pushing through the crowd. The angry murmuring began to die.

Watching, Adni realized she would have to do more.

As Cockram mounted the steps and banged on the door of the mansion, shouting about souls and salvation, corruption and manipulation, Adni sidled up to a man who stood alone at the edge of the crowd. He was still under the thrall of the spell that hung in the air. It pressed on Adni's mind as well, but she held herself apart from it.

She reached out from under her cloak, setting her hand on the man's arm. "He's lying," she said. "He's been wrong about everything. He's a dangerous man." As she spoke, she wove a subtle passive persuasion spell. She let it go, felt it settle into place, and moved on to the woman standing next to him.

Adni kept it up. She was weaker than she might have been, thanks to the distance between herself and Bol. If she'd have known she'd be casting so much, she'd have brought him with her.

Still, as she spoke the same words to the woman, wove a spell, and stepped on, she thought it would be enough. The crowd was more inclined to believe the evidence they'd all seen themselves—Cockram defending himself via a dome of shimmering magic—than his feeble efforts to shift the blame.

As Cockram banged on the door again, his voice growing frantic as he shouted about the truth and the rector and Delari's hope for mankind, Adni touched arm after arm, letting weaving after weaving settle over the people gathered on the lawn. She experimented with touching two people at once while targeting them with the same spell. She grew more adept as she moved, and she kept it up until she was, at last, exhausted. She drew off to the side, woozy with her exertions.

She looked up at Cockram. He was on the stoop, heaving himself bodily against the door. But it was sturdy, and he was not.

Adni stood a while longer, breathing in the bitter smoke of the torches, until, at last, she felt the spell containing the crowd fail. She felt it happen, felt the way it cut off at the base and began to unravel, inch by inch.

The crowd stirred. Men blinked and shook themselves, women whispered to one another. All of them knew the same thing now.

Adni watched, a smile playing on her lips. She knew what every person in that crowd was thinking. *He's lying. He's been wrong about everything. He's a dangerous man.*

And the best part was, it was all true.

The mob began to wake up. Raised voices all spoke the same words. Cockram tried to speak, to shout them down. But it was no use.

It was dark and quiet down by the warmlake. It was a relief, being away from the city. Tassin had led them out a side gate in the wall, then unerringly over grassy slopes towards the water.

They'd gone straight out onto a spit of sand, where he'd collected Tibs. Nel was there too, hauling her smooth body out of the shallows, heaving towards Embriem's round-toed boot. But Embriem hadn't even looked at his brinlin until Marim said to him in a low hiss, "Go on, then. Pick her up."

He picked her up in a movement so mechanical it made Marim's heart turn over in her chest. She caught Braven casting a glance at her, his eyes wary. He seemed to be keeping a certain distance away from her, as if he didn't entirely trust she wouldn't do the same thing to him

She wanted to explain. She wanted to tell him she had almost no experience with persuasion, and had maybe pushed a little too hard. She wanted to tell him about the academy and how she'd never been much good at anything except healing. She wanted to tell him the only reason she'd graduated at all was because everyone felt sorry for her.

But she also didn't want to tell him. He was looking at her as if he thought her capable of wielding all kinds of violent magics. Better, perhaps, not to dispel that myth until she knew more about where they were going.

Tassin, murmuring to his brinlin in a soothing tone, tucked Tibs into his shirt collar. Embriem held Nel woodenly in his hand. Braven said, "This way. Hurry. A little ways up the shore."

They walked in silence. Marim stumbled after Braven and the boy, weighed down by her heavy bag, Embriem on her heels.

There was no path, and the grass was high, the soil lumpy underneath. No one seemed to notice her struggling.

Finally she wheeled on Embriem and said, "Carry this. Careful, though. Let Nel ride in your collar"

Embriem took the bag from her, heaved it onto his own shoulder, and looked at her with the blank expectant expression of a loyal dog. "Delari's breath," Marim swore, "this is so creepy."

Braven was looking at her again, that apprehensive stare. But before she could say anything he was moving again, his body a shifting smudge in his dark cloak.

When they stopped again, it was next to a stand of reeds. It was indistinguishable, as far as Marim could tell, from the dozens of other stands they'd passed as they traversed along the lakeshore. Only here, Braven shouldered his way into the tall plants, pushing the stalks aside and making his way along a path that was angled in such a way as to be all but invisible from the shore.

Tassin paused to look back at Marim. She nodded, and he went ahead. Marim went next, Embriem stumping along behind her.

Then they were in the water, the shallows lapping up to soak her boots and seep into her skirts. She heard Braven's voice telling Tassin to hop in, and then she found herself faced with a boat.

It was a narrow, slim vessel, with barely room for four people to ride. It was a task, loading themselves and the ungainly bag. Marim ended up in the bottom with her sea bag in her lap

At last, they were all situated, and Braven began to row. He piloted the craft up the lake, into the silent, whispering fog. In the distance, the sky above Lan Dinas still glowed.

The night seemed to close in around them. The lap of water and the cries of the brinlins in the reeds were the only sounds. Sitting awkwardly, her back pressed up against Embriem's legs, Marim felt strangely restless. She fiddled with her sea bag, working the tie on the top.

She'd left the tablet box on top. Never again, she decided, would she travel without it on her person. Never would she risk being so separated from the people she loved. Now, in the moonlit darkness, she pulled the box free and undid the latch.

The first two tablets, the one with the academy's seal, the other with Professor Liam's chop, were blank. She could see the smooth leather, unbroken by the score of the scribis.

The third bore a message. It was only three words, but they sent a shiver up Marim's spine.

"I am coming."

Excerpt from

BRINLIN COVE

Annals of the Brinlocks: Book III

A Story of Bydaira

Robin Stephen

Prelude

Of all the things Marim feared, this moment was straight out of her nightmares.

She stood on the jagged spine of the summit of Cynnes Tarth, the fog livid and torn around her. Below her, the ancient forest was on fire. She could see the lurid glow even through the haze. Above her, the sky was murderous. Lightning raked the heavens in forks of writhing brilliance.

And she'd just watched her best friend fall to his death.

It was over. Their plan had failed. Up ahead, the massive, cracked globe that marked the summit of Cynnes Tarth flickered in and out of view with the flashing sky, spewing showers of sparks from its cracked surface. Behind her, Vailria lay as still as a corpse.

Marim wanted to rewind time, to go back five minutes and argue harder, make herself heard, make herself listened to.

It was too late. Marim felt stunned. She was shivering, but she hardly felt the cold rain. She had the vague impression someone was speaking to her, but she could not stop staring at the shifting fog, the craggy rocks up ahead.

With a sense of numb disbelief, she thought of all the steps that had led to this moment. Every link in the chain seemed so unlikely in retrospect. It seemed impossible she'd ever left Masidon in the first place, that she'd been put off her ship and left behind in Lan Dinas, that she'd stumbled upon Tassin and unlocked the secret of the Brinlocks.

Back at the academy, so many of the students had lofty goals. With the new strains of tessili seeming to manifest more and more powerful skills with each new bonding, there was excitement in every department. Long lost skills were being rediscovered, ancient magics coming alive in the world again.

Marim had never been ambitious. She'd never had any reason to think she would accomplish something grand or significant. Kix was nothing special, and neither was she. That had been clear enough from the beginning.

And yet, she always seemed to end up in these moments: these situations where she triggered something large, something terrible, something she could not contain again once it had been turned loose.

She could not go back in time and make different decisions, no matter how hard she wished to. Feeling the weight of all her mistakes mounting to an unbearable pressure, she thought how much easier it would be if she never came down from this mountain either. Surely the Brinlocks would blame her, and rightly, for this terrible storm. If anyone survived, they would demand justice.

If I die, I can't harm anybody else.

Marim took a step closer to the edge. Kix, anxious, prodded her neck with his cold, sharp nose. It was too bad she could not die without killing her tessila as well. She felt a pang for that betrayal.

Someone was speaking her name, but the idea of tumbling into oblivion was alluring in its simplicity. It filled her mind, leaving no room for any other thought, any other sensation.

It was the best way, the best thing to do.

She glanced one final time towards the cracked orb, straining to make out the uneven rocks in front of it, just in case. But he was not there. He had fallen. She'd seen him fall.

Well. He had been more talented than her by any measure. In this one thing, she could be his match.

She took another step and drew in a final breath, prepared to fling herself off the side of the mountain.

Chapter 1

Marim ground to a stop, panting. She could see only a few feet up the slope before the trail ahead of her was swallowed by the inevitable fog. It could be another mile to the top of the climb, for all she knew.

She tried to rally, but her legs felt like butter left out in the sun. She was hungry, too. The air up here was thin and stimulating. She'd been feeling a growl in her belly for the last hour.

Giving up, Marim flopped down on a boulder, unslung her pack from her shoulders, and called ahead. "I'm taking a break."

She situated herself on the slope. If not for the fog, she imagined she'd have a spectacular view. They'd climbed high enough this morning that the trees had changed. Instead of the towering, ancient sentinels that surrounded Gol Ledrith, these were skinny pines. The scent of their needles was a sharp snap on the wispy air.

But still, the fog. It clung to the slopes of these jagged mountains just as tenaciously as it did the fertile plains around the city of Lan Dinas, where Marim had lived for half a year after arriving here on Cynnes Tarth, the largest of the Fog Isles.

In the nine months since she'd fled the city and followed a stranger into the heart of the forest, it seemed everything had changed. For one thing, Marim was finding the fog—never her favorite feature of this place to begin with—more irritating than ever.

Settling her pack in her lap, Marim opened the leather flap and drew out the packet of cured meat and the little skin of sweet tea she'd brought with her. A moment later, she heard the scuff of light footsteps running back down the stone path. She looked up as Tassin materialized out of the mist, his faced flushed with exercise, eyes alight with the thrill of exploration. "Braven says we're almost there now."

Marim didn't move. She began to unwrap the packet of meat. "Braven's been saying that for the last two hours. I'm resting here."

Tassin stood a moment, rocking onto his toes and glancing back up the narrow trail they'd been following since dawn. He'd sprouted several inches of height since summer, and his face had taken on a new look of maturity. Looking at him, Marim felt a twinge of guilt. It was good to see him happy for once, distracted from the weight of worry he hadn't been able to put aside since the night he, Marim, and his father had fled from an angry mob.

The boy chewed his lip, eyeing the meats. "It's really true this time though. I got up above the fog myself. It happens just ahead. We were there waiting on these benches up there when we heard you say you were stopping."

Marim paused, the tantalizing spice of the meats rich in her nose. She supposed it was her own fault. She should have known better than to set out on a tough trail with Braven and Tassin for her companions. Tassin had the boundless energy of a growing child, and Braven had spent his entire life walking these forests and slopes.

With poor grace, Marim gave in. She rewrapped the meats and replaced the packet in her bag with the skin. She hauled herself to her feet and looked at Tassin, who grinned and turned to hurry back up the trail on light feet. Within moments, he'd disappeared again.

It was one of the strangest things about the fog. It could make you feel entirely alone even when there were people all around. And the problem with being alone was the way it left you with time and space to think.

Marim felt she'd spent entirely too much time thinking since she'd left Lan Dinas and come to Gol Ledrith. She thought about Embriem and what she'd done to him. She thought about the ship that was coming, bearing Coll as well as a formal delegation of Tessilari sent by the King and Queen of Masidon to make contact with the Brinlocks – the hidden race that had persisted here on this island for centuries, concealed from the world and utterly forgotten until Marim had unwittingly let the news out.

It had seemed exciting, at the time. The discovery of another people, similar to the Tessilari but different as well. It had never occurred to her not to share what she was learning about the brinlins with her contacts back at the academy. She hadn't taken time to consider the consequences. It seemed to Marim she'd done a lot of that in the last few years – setting out on a course of action without properly taking time to anticipate where it would lead.

The trail grew steeper as the pines fell away, leaving Marim feeling like she was balancing on a disembodied bit of stone surrounded on all sides by nothing but shifting, fog-filled air. A sense of vertigo swept over her. She reached out to trail her fingers along the rough stone of the slope to her right to reassure herself she was still in contact with the earth.

Then, from one step to the next, the fog grew thinner, thinner, and was gone. Marim blinked as brilliant, unfiltered sunlight fell full on her face for what seemed the first time in years. She looked ahead to see Embriem and Tassin a small distance away, seated in a kind of stone crow's nest with high-backed benches carved into the rock and a little table at its center. Braven had set out cheeses, more meats, a loaf of dark bread, and three flagons. He lifted one when he saw Marim, a grin splitting his friendly face. The young Keeper's straw-colored hair was damp and rumpled, but otherwise he appeared not at all affected by the long climb. "You made it. Hooray."

Behind the stone table and benches, Marim could see the peak of Cynnes Tarth. It reared up behind them, growing steeper and more craggy until it ended in a jagged slab of granite inscribed with runes. Carved into the rough summit sat a massive globe of stone, its surface utterly smooth except for a crack that ran through its center. The smooth sphere lay nestled as if cupped by the mountain itself, huge and looming even from this distance. Most of the runes around it were dark, but one or two glowed with a wan, feeble light.

Still a little unsteady on her feet, Marim hurried to the bench. She flopped herself onto the cool seat, setting her pack down beside her. Braven, still smiling, nudged a flagon in her direction. Marim suddenly wondered how she looked. Her face must be flushed, and she'd opened her collar an hour or two before, feeling too stifled to leave it in place. Now she buttoned it back up and made an attempt to smooth her spikey hair as Kix wheeled in from above and landed on her shoulder to strut about and hiss at Braven.

Sitting, Marim at last had a moment to take in the view, and it was every bit as astonishing as Braven had promised.

Below them lay the island of Cynnes Tarth, the details of its geography and shoreline obscured under the heavy bank of fog that hung over the land like a pale umbrella. Beyond the fog, however, the brilliant sea glittered under the sun, stretching away to meet a blank horizon on all sides but one. To the north, Marim could see the humped shapes of the other islands, each one shrouded in mist.

Braven took a sip from his flagon, his eyes brilliant as emeralds as he took in the view. "It's a good day to come. Very clear. Sometimes the fog covers the ocean, too."

They'd come up the slope from the south. Now, as she caught her breath, Marim leaned over a little, looking down the other side at the steep descent, wishing the fog would clear off so she could see what lay below. According to Braven, there was an ancient, abandoned city there, built in a sheltered cove, ringed by jagged cliffs on one side and sandy, smooth beaches on the other. It was a place he thought the ship from Masidon might be able to put in so as not to risk the hostile reception it would likely receive in Lan Dinas.

It had seemed a hopeful thing, when Braven had first mentioned the cove. Now, sitting in the sun and feeling the cool, clear air dry the sweat off her skin, Marim wasn't so sure. This would be a difficult climb to subject the Tessilari to, with any luggage they might have brought and all the different kinds of people that could be expected to attend diplomats on a mission of importance.

Marim picked up her own flagon and took a sip of the light, foamy brew the Brinlocks called tiin and drank like water though it was mildly alcoholic. Resolutely, she pulled her mind away from her troubles. They'd learn whether or not the cove would be the answer to her problem soon enough.

To distract herself, she turned again to look at the massive, rearing stone orb with its cracked surface and the runes carved around its base. "What's that?" She jutted her chin at the summit.

Braven glanced at the orb with an air of unease. "There are things like that all over the island. Leftovers from before." He shrugged and cut a sliver off one of the cheeses.

"Before what?" The tiin was going straight to Marim's head, which wasn't great considering the descent they would need to make after they ate. The last thing she needed was to break her back tumbling down some long slope. She set the flagon aside in favor of her tea.

Braven flicked invisible crumbs off his cloak as his mouth compressed into an unhappy line. Watching him, she felt a surge of gratitude for his easy-going company. She'd been among the Brinlocks for nine months now, and he was the only one who'd befriended her.

There was a long pause, as if Braven was weighing various possible responses and finding them all lacking. Finally, he looked back at her. His green eyes were grave. "Like the Tessilari, the Brinlocks sacrificed much in exchange for safety. What few secrets we have left, we keep."

It had been years since Braven last made the trek over the mountain. As a boy, he'd come this way often, sometimes bringing a pack and camping out in one of the empty houses in the cove. At first, it was just a place to be alone, to withdraw from the rowdiness of the other boys and his crowded house. As he grew older, though, it became something more than that.

The elegant buildings spoke to him. The way they grew out of the very stone of the cliffs had its own silent poetry. He began to study the buildings, the way homes were connected with stone paths and bridges over canals that must have once carried water. At first, he assumed that water would have come from the sea. But after searching along the entire extent of the sandy beach, he never found a mouth of any kind. None of the canals extended so low as to come anywhere near the tide, even when it was high.

That got him thinking. The next time Braven visited the abandoned city, he came with a roll of paper and a stick of drawing coal. He began mapping the canals, tracing their origins. Gradually he discovered they all connected back to one place, combining in a great cistern that ran beneath a massive stone covered in unlit runes and disappeared beneath the mountain.

He'd dropped into the dark place beneath the boulder and walked into the dusty darkness. Dried leaves and fallen debris rustling with his every step, he'd walked back and down, back and down on an ever-descending slope until the light at the mouth was only a tiny square in the distance. So far beneath so much stone, he'd lost his nerve listening to the way his own breath echoed against the stone walls. Too spooked to go further, he'd scrambled back out into the light. Outside, he'd stood and craned his neck, looking up at the towering peak of the mountain. How deep did it go? And why was it dry?

As a teenager, he'd developed a theory. He came to believe the canals had once connected to the warmlake. Water had been pulled through the mountain and into the beautiful city so

Brinlocks could live there, their brinlins free to come and go as they pleased. He could well imagine what the city must have looked like full of people, the canals alight with glittering water, stands of reeds growing in the round pools set at intervals throughout the city. He became convinced this was the solution to the overpopulation problem that had everyone so worried.

The more he thought about it, the more it made sense. Why risk populating downstream, drawing closer to the edge of the wood where they might be discovered? Why not instead re-activate the ancient canal system? As soon as they did, they'd have a pre-made city twice the size of Gol Ledrith to move into, one even more secure and isolated.

For months, Braven had haunted the abandoned city like a ghost, enchanted with his idea. He'd grown so excited, so convinced he'd uncovered a secret, he eventually requested an audience with the Wheel to explain his plan for fixing everything.

Even now, over a decade later, Braven felt a flush of embarrassment when he remembered the way he'd strode into the audience chamber and spread his crude maps on the applicant's table. He'd stood there, puffed up with the pride of his discovery, and explained how all that was needed was a crew to go into the canal tunnel and excavate a way back to the lake. Then they'd need a few talented casters to work out how to reactive the old runes that had once filled the city with water. He extrapolated at some length on his theory about how Brinlocks had made those carved stone buildings and lived there, enjoying the splendid view of the cove and the expansive beaches.

He'd stopped speaking at last, and waited for a response. During formal hearings, all the members of the Wheel sat behind screens, each within a bubble of magic that distorted the voice, making it impossible to recognize which individual member might be addressing the chamber. Braven stood with his chin raised, expecting to be praised and made much of.

Instead, a resonate voice made eerie by the distortion responded from behind a screen to his right. "The decision to abandon Carreg Dinas was not made lightly. It was done in a time of crisis. Much was sacrificed to hide us then, so we could withdraw from the world and escape the fate that befell our cousins. Shifting the shape of the island was difficult, and those who gave their strength to this work sacrificed everything to keep us, their descendants, safe. For hundreds of years, we have abided here in Gol Ledrith, and we have prospered."

There was a pause. Braven felt a dip of disbelief, felt the blood rush to his face. He had felt, all this time, the city was his somehow: its secrets unexplored. Why had it never occurred him to ask an elder about its history?

The voice continued, speaking in a slow, measured tone. "You are not the first to make this proposal. Some even on this Wheel believe the broken channel should be repaired. But I ask you, young Braven, what will happen to the houses in Gol Ledrith when the water level of the lake drops to fill those canals? Are you willing to risk the possibility we may have to abandon our homes here? How will we patrol the forest if a mountain stands between its slopes and our dwellings? And finally, what of the old, broken magic that lives even now in the mountain, calling down storms when the seasons change and causing them to linger here? Some who have studied the remnants of the old spells believe any strengthening of the flow of magic through the mountain would bring disaster down upon us in the shape of storms far worse than those we endure now."

It had gone on like that for some time. One after another, voices rose up from behind the screens, explaining all the risks of what Braven proposed to do. There was no anger in the voices, no scorn. Only the multitude of considerations he had overlooked.

When he'd been allowed to leave at last, he'd taken the maps he'd so painstakingly created and thrown them into the warmlake. Then he'd run off into the forest, half hoping he'd step on an adder just so he'd have something else to think about.

Since that day, Braven had never returned to the broken city of Carreg Dinas. But now, as he led Marim down the stone path cut into the side of the mountain, the place took his breath away as surely as it ever had in his boyhood. They descended past the stepped buildings, walking across the delicate arched bridges, gazed down into the dusty canals. He led her through the central square, where carved benches sat positioned around a large, empty pool. He tried to pretend he didn't notice the way her eyes lingered on the seats. He knew she wanted to rest. But he also knew they needed to hurry if they hoped to make it to their destination and then back over the cliffs and off the steep part of the mountain to the holding pen where they'd left the horses before the light began to fail.

He kept up a brisk walk. They shuffled through the abandoned city, three tiny figures on streets made for hundreds. They reached the seawall with the stone quay and continued on. The fog was thinner on this side of the mountain. Braven could see the white sand of the beach below, the glitter of water beyond.

Marim paused to look, but he kept going. He led her along the docks and onto the little jut of the land with a narrow path grooved into the stone. The salt was heavy on the air now, the wind from the sea a playful hand in his hair.

The trail took an upwards path that ended, at last, in a stony outcropping above the sea. Below lay the cove's mouth – a narrow channel between jagged cliffs. Braven stopped and pointed. "Here. It's the only way in. Do you think a ship could get through?" He had to raise his voice to make it carry over the crash and thunder of the surf below.

Braven knew nothing about seafaring. He'd seen ships, of course, but only from a distance. To him, they were tiny black specks that inched over the brilliant ocean like ants crawling up a boulder. Now, looking at Marim, he saw her face fall.

The mountains that encircled this cove formed almost a complete circle. They were broken only in this one place where the sea spilled in. The mouth itself was wide, but five massive spires of jagged rock jutted up out of the water at intervals, leaving only narrow channels of open water between them. There were runes on the spires, and they glowed with a quiet, pale light.

Looking at Marim, Braven could see he'd been wrong. A ship could not pass into this place. The stone spires blocked the way.

And the fog seemed especially thick right around the mouth of the cove, an impenetrable bank that made it impossible to see where water ended and stone began.

They stood a moment. Braven could see the sag in Marim's shoulders. The hope that had been fueling her was spent, leaving her exhausted.

Still, she tried to rally. "Maybe they could tie up on the other side of those rocks," she said, "and row in with lifeboats."

But she didn't sound hopeful. The sea was restless here. With the fog and the chop, even Braven could see it would be a dangerous passage. One errant wave could smash a small boat against one of the stone pillars.

He felt foolish again, like he had when he'd taken his proposal to the Wheel. At least this time, it hadn't been his idea. He'd mentioned this place when Marim had asked if he knew of anywhere but Lan Dinas where a ship might land. He'd told her of the abandoned city, its silent docks. Since then, she hadn't let it drop. She'd pestered and badgered until, at last, he'd consented to bring her here.

Now, feeling the sour residue of disappointment, the three of them stood in silence, the thick, salty air rough against their faces. Tassin, standing on the edge of the outcropping, observed in a subdued voice, "Funny how they're all so evenly spaced, and so alike. The five big rocks, I mean."

+

Embriem looked up as a key turned in the lock, a frantic hope igniting in his chest. He sat up straighter in his padded chair, which was arranged for a view of the lake outside. He turned, straining to see who had come.

When he saw the familiar tousled head poke around the door, Embriem's hope died. The energy that had come into him for a moment drained away. He sagged back against his pillows and fixed his eyes once more on the window, no longer interested in anything.

He listened as Tassin and the grizzled man who held the keys to Embriem's prison exchanged a few sentences. The man said, "Just shout if you need anything, lad." Then came the sound of the door closing again, the latch turning.

Embriem closed his eyes. The pain, briefly obscured by hope, rose up again. Hard and sharp, it seemed to stab within his temples. Her voice echoed in the quiet reaches of his mind. *Come with me, Embriem. Now.*

But how could he go with her when he was kept locked up like a thief? It wasn't his fault he couldn't obey.

But the pain didn't care about intentions. It rewarded only action.

Tassin moved across the room on light feet. He sat down in the chair across from his father's and said hello in a tone of false cheerfulness. When Embriem made no response, his son sat in silence for a moment before continuing to speak in a dogged tone, his expression determined. "We went to the abandoned city today and saw the cove. Some of the houses are huge, and you know what? They're carved right into the cliffs and the mountainside."

Embriem opened his eyes, the bright pain shifting. "Marim? Did she go with you?" Just speaking her name gave him a little thrill of pleasure, but it also made the pain stir and come forward, shifting and stabbing.

Tassin's expression went carefully blank. He turned to look at the deepening dusk outside the window. "She'll come see you soon, father. I'm sure."

It was not wasted on Embriem that Tassin didn't answer his question. His son had developed an evasive side of his character lately that Embriem did not like. He closed his eyes again.

Giving up, Tassin rose. He walked to the trough that carried water into the room from the warmlake. In one corner, it widened out into an elevated pond where reeds grew and the water swirled in a lazy current, steam rising off the surface. "And how is Nel today?"

Embriem didn't answer. Nel was how she'd been for months – disengaged and listless, perched on a reed. Her light blue hide with its silver speckles was going scaly from lack of time spent in the water. Her eyes had a glazed look to them. Normally, a brinlin would never allow itself to be touched by any human it wasn't bound to. Now, Tassin crossed the room and gently scooped her small body into his hand.

Embriem didn't watch. He knew the routine. Tassin did this daily, at least three times, sometimes as many as five. The boy lowered his hand into the water, submerging Nel so the life-granting waters of the warmlake could replenish her energy and her hide. He scratched her under the chin, eliciting a small sound that was indicative neither of pleasure or pain. Then he reached up and broke off one of the narrow pods that grew on the reeds, cracked it open, and fed Nel one soft, buttery seed after another. She took them. Though her response was listless, she chewed them down. Tassin kept up until she turned her blunt face away and refused to continue eating.

Midway through the process, there was a disruption on the other side of the small pond. Tibs erupted out of the water, gills flared to gulp air. Embriem knew Tassin left his own brinlin far out in the warmlake each time he intended to attend to Nel, to give himself more time.

As Tibs burst out of the water, hissing and mewling with anger, Tassin spoke in a sharp, annoyed tone. "Calm down, Tibs. Sit there and wait. I'll be done in a moment."

Embriem wasn't watching, but he could imagine the sullen slink as the brilliant orange brinlin with her blue spots climbed up a reed and watched Tassin feeding Nel with smoldering, jealous eyes. No matter how many times Tassin did this, Tibs never grew easier about the process, never learned to take it in stride. Had Embriem not been too full of pain to care about anything, he might have found that interesting.

Instead, he leaned his head back against the cushions and listened to Tibs' unhappy keen until Tassin, at last, had to give in, withdraw Nel from the water and set her back on her reed. He scooped Tibs up in his hand and, without another word for his father, stalked into his own room. The boy slammed his door with unnecessary force.

Embriem drew in a breath as silence and pain combined in his system like a cruel sedative. He told himself Tassin wasn't wholly to blame for his temper. Just like Tassin and Tibs, Embriem and Nel were connected. It was, in part, his brinlin's malaise that infected Embriem, making the prospect of getting out of this chair, of caring about anything but Marim, impossible.

Outside, night continued to fall. Darkness gathered, and Embriem sat with his eyes closed. He supposed they would bring food soon, like they did twice a day, and leave it sitting by him until the gnawing hunger in his belly roused him enough to take a few bites. Still, when he heard the key in the lock again, he couldn't help but feel that spark of hope, couldn't resist turning to look.

It wasn't the stout woman who brought his meals morning and night. It wasn't he man who guarded the door. It wasn't the smooth-faced healer who prodded him with questions. And it wasn't Marim.

It was someone else entirely.

The figure that walked into the room was a tall man, much taller than Embriem, with a lean frame and hooded, colorless eyes. Quite a few Brinlocks had been to see Embriem in the months he'd been shut in this apartment, but Embriem didn't think he'd seen this one before.

He didn't care. He lay back, a feeling of exhaustion billowing through him. He closed his eyes, not even interested enough to watch as the man moved across the room and settled into the chair Tassin had vacated a short time before. He spoke in a clear, resonant tone. "Hello, Embriem. My name is Aldrath, and I am Master of Magics here in Gol Ledrith. I'd have come to you sooner, but I've been away."

Embriem did not respond. The man settled himself in the chair, smoothing his dark robes with a quiet rustle. He carried with him the spicy scent of the fog. He let a few beats pass in silence, then spoke again. "I hear you are the victim of an active persuasion spell."

This time, the words penetrated the fog of pain. The word "victim" set off a little spark of anger, and Embriem's eyes slid open of their own accord. He looked at the man, took in the deep lines of his face, the silver and green brinlin clinging just within the cowl of his robe's hood. "If you've come to help, tell that man at the door to stand aside."

A look flickered over the man's face. Regret? Annoyance? Embriem couldn't tell, didn't care. His visitor leaned back in his chair and steepled his fingers before his face. "I do hope to be able to do that one day. For now, though, I must ask you a few questions."

✛

Solitude was not a problem for Vailria. All her life, she'd been alone. As a child, she'd been alone in her fascinations. She never liked the way other children played, so she'd played by herself.

As a teenager, she'd had a brief respite: a heady season of love and returned affection, a glimpse of a union and a future. But that hadn't lasted, and afterwards she'd been alone in her grief, alone with her terrible memories of the day her first love died. Her tragedy had set her apart from her peers, who couldn't understand what she'd lost. And it had set her apart from her elders, who seemed to believe she would recover quickly because she was young.

But what had happened that day still haunted her.

They'd been strolling along the lakeshore, holding hands. One moment he'd been perfectly fine – a straight, strong young man, full of laughter and life. She'd been in love with him, and this knowledge had made her existence both simple and happy in a way it never had been before.

Then, with no warning, her lover had pitched forward and fallen hard, collapsing onto the pebbled shore like a tossed bag of flour. She'd rolled him over, seen his blank eyes, and screamed.

She never learned what had killed his brinlin. It happened that way sometimes. Out in the lake, a fisher bird perhaps, or a predatory fish, had made an unlucky kill. There was no way to know the details.

For a long time after, Vailria had been alone because she could not abide the company of other people, couldn't bear to risk another loss. Eventually this predilection for solitude led her to train for the isolated position of a Watcher, and apply for the position outside Lan Dinas. Finally, she'd been alone in the physical sense, passing the days in her little house without company of either Brinlock or human.

Then she'd met Tommin. Young and full of dreams, he was newly arrived from one of the outer islands, and they'd been enchanted with one another from the beginning. For six months, she'd been blissfully happy. They'd spent endless hours together while his ship grew in the drydocks.

She'd known all along it was temporary. They were of an age, but he was to become a sea captain, his feet destined to spend more time on the deck of a ship than on dry land. But at least he was no Brinlock. Vailria found this comforting. He was a strong young man, and his life was linked to nothing but her. For the second time in Vailria's life, she'd been happy.

Then, Tommin had left. He'd wanted to take her with him. She'd had to explain why she could not go, entrusting him with her secret, enduring his disbelief and sadness, then watching him sail away.

He came back, though. Every time he made the dangerous crossing to and from Masidon, Tommin stopped in Lan Dinas to restock and refit his vessel, to sell the valuable goods he'd picked up on the distant continent. At least, when his ship was in port, they were together.

When Tommin returned to Lan Dinas one spring and told her of the tiny island he'd found off the tip of Cynnes Tarth, habitable but surrounded by submerged reefs and thus difficult to approach, she'd been only mildly interested. She'd listened as he described the bright white beach, the humped hills, the fertile expanse of flat land in the island's center and, most importantly, the tiny little warmlake, complete with a population of brinlins and local fog bank.

She'd asked a question or two, and he'd grown excited. This place, he told her, was their ticket to a life together. They could escape to their own private paradise. She would no longer have to live on the fringes of two cultures, keeping secrets from both. He would no longer have to risk the dangerous passage to Masidon. He would make enough runs, stashing his profits. In a few years, he'd be able to afford timber for a house and some livestock. He'd sell the ship and its valuable guide globe, pay off his investors, and buy a light sailboat. The two of them would be free of their respective responsibilities. They could be together, be themselves, at last.

Vailria had never entirely taken the plan seriously. Even as, one visit after another, Tommin told her about his visits to the island, the way he was getting more familiar with the reef, the supply caches he was building up, the chickens he'd turned loose, in the back of her mind she'd been convinced it wouldn't happen. It had been her way of defending against hope.

But now, somehow, she was here.

Someday, Tommin assured her, they would have a proper house. It would have a deck that extended over the warmlake, with portholes in the floor and reeds in the living room, just like she wanted. Tok would never be far from her, and neither would Tommin. He'd be back in just a few weeks, with some goras and plenty of seeds for the garden and a small vessel he could manage without a crew.

That's what he'd said six months ago, anyway, when he'd left in the rowboat on his way back to the ship. She'd still been weak then, for Tok had nearly died on the journey here.

It wasn't they'd had far to come. She could see the craggy shoulders of Cynnes Tarth from the white beach Tommin had first described to her so long ago. It was the reef that surrounded this place that made the approach so treacherous. No vessel could make it through except in the calmest of seas. They'd had to wait weeks for the right conditions. The time away from a warmlake had taken its toll on Tok, and thus on her.

Now, Vailria was stronger again. But she was alone. Very, very alone.

At first, she hadn't minded. Tommin had set cornerstones for the foundation of the house. He'd left her with tools, and she'd set about doing what she could. She put in garden beds. She harvested reed stalks and wove a clumsy henhouse for the chickens. She collected reed roots and brewed tiin. And every day, she walked across the sandy beach and climbed the stone outcropping to the highest point of the island. She stared at the horizon until her eyes ached, straining for a glimpse of a vessel that was not there.

One month had passed, then another, and another. Now it was a week into the fourth month, and Vailria was growing worried. Tok was mostly recovered from the terrible depletion he'd suffered from being away from a warmlake for so long. Though he missed the brinlins he'd liked to swim with in Cynnes Tarth, he'd made some new friends now.

As his vitality renewed itself, so did Vailria's energy. The days, she found, were long. There was a little fog here, clinging over the lake, but not enough to reach much past the edge of the water. The sky was usually clear during the long months of summer, and Vailria could watch the sun crawl its slow, slow progress across the sky.

It was in the second month she began to feel truly alone. It wasn't the lack of company that bothered her, more the realization that if something happened to Tommin, she would be stranded. No one back in Gol Ledrith knew where she'd gone. For his part, Tommin had kept this place a secret. No one would ever come looking for her here.

And that knowledge didn't lie so easy in Vailria's mind. She was used to being alone, yes, but could she really be content never seeing another human again for the rest of her life? How long would that life be if she had no company, no partner? Vailria could do many things, but building a house would be difficult without the materials Tommin had planned to bring back with him. The tent she lived in, pitched on the lakeshore, was adequate. But it would hardly offer sufficient protection again the sorts of violent storms that moved through these waters when the seasons changed.

Every day, she found herself wondering what had happened back in Gol Ledrith the night they'd fled. Had the riot spread? Were Embriem and his son safe? Or had something terrible happened?

At first, when Vailria's thoughts strayed in this direction, she told herself they deserved whatever befell them. They had rejected her advice, after all, and refused to follow her to safety when they'd had the chance.

Day by day, however, this argument rang a little more hollow in her own head. She hadn't, after all, given them a chance. She'd come in with her spells, pushing, driven by her sense of urgency. She hadn't taken time to explain, to persuade. She'd become too accustomed to her own power, too comfortable with setting her fingertips lightly on a man's arm and having him suddenly see things her way.

As the days passed and still Tommin did not return, Vailria found herself wondering if she'd made the right decision.

One morning she woke to find a chicken dead, throat torn, feathers scattered all over what she'd come to think of as her yard. After that, she set to weaving a spell into a low fence to keep anything that wasn't welcome outside its boundary. It wasn't anything formidable enough to work on a man, but it might keep the sea foxes, with their sharp teeth and slick, slinking bodies, at bay.

And finally, one day she looked out on the horizon and saw it was not empty. Squinting into the sun, she wove a small spell, cupping the air in her palm to form a looking orb.

The ship was no small craft like the one Tommin intended to bring back with him. It was a towering thing, every bit as massive as Tommin's trade vessel. Its many masts bristled like a small, floating forest, and its sails bore a crest even Vailria recognized.

She lowered her hand, feeling a strange stillness settle on her heart. In the distance, behind the ship, she could see the fog capped cliffs of Cynnes Tarth.

The Tessilari had found the Brinlocks at last.

KEEP READING
http://robinstephen.com/brinlincove

FREE GIFT

Thank you for reading *Brinlin Forest,* the second installment in *Annals of the Brinlocks.* If you enjoyed the book, you might like to join Robin Stephen's mailing list. You'll get some exclusive Bydaira content for free, just for signing up.

To learn more, visit robinstephen.com/free

BOOKS BY ROBIN STEPHEN

Chronicles of the Tessilari
Tessili Academy
Tessili Rogue
Tessili Revenge

Annals of the Brinlocks
Brinlin Isle
Brinlin Forest
Brinlin Cove